Hamilton Aïdé

A Voyage of Discovery - A Novel of American Society

Vol. I

Hamilton Aïdé

A Voyage of Discovery - A Novel of American Society
Vol. I

ISBN/EAN: 9783337040345

Printed in Europe, USA, Canada, Australia, Japan

Cover: Foto ©Andreas Hilbeck / pixelio.de

More available books at **www.hansebooks.com**

A

VOYAGE OF DISCOVERY

A Novel of American Society

BY

Hamilton Aïdé

IN TWO VOLUMES

VOL. I.

LONDON

JAMES R. OSGOOD, McILVAINE & CO.

45, ALBEMARLE STREET, W.

1892

TO MY DEAR COMPANIONS

ON

A VOYAGE OF DISCOVERY

I dedicate these pages.

A VOYAGE OF DISCOVERY.

CHAPTER I.

" WHY are you going to the United States ? "
asked an American, no longer in his first
youth, of a young Englishwoman on board the
Teutonic, the second day after they had left
Liverpool.

The sky was blue, the sea was smooth,
the hour was noon. The lady was stretched
on a deck-chair, the American sat beside
her. Both were fine types of their races,
both had faces which arrested and held
the attention. Mr. Quintin Ferrars was unusually tall for an American, his limbs were not
loosely knit, and his walk was erect and firm,
attributes more common to the dwellers in the
prairie than to those on the Fifth Avenue.

He had a resolute, thoughtful face, over which
gleams of satire were more apt to play than
those of sympathy, with keen eyes, the expression, even the colour, of which it was difficult
to determine.   Neither in his accent nor in
his colloquialisms was there any touch of the
peculiarity which we call "American," but
which our cousins affirm to be drawn through
conduits of heredity from the undefiled well
of English speech of their Puritan fathers.
Mr. Ferrars was accused of being an Anglomaniac ; it would be more true to say that he
was keenly critical of the defects in his own
country.   But, then, he was critical of all things
human and divine.

The young Englishwoman, in her tight-fitting
ulster of russet tweed, with a stalking cap of
the same material, beneath which her abundant
auburn hair was tightly rolled, was tall and had
a well-balanced figure, with a waist sufficiently
large to support her breadth of shoulder and
finely-developed bust, without suggesting a
fear that it might snap in two.   Her clear
grey eyes under dark, level brows, had a singular directness of outlook ; the fine lines of
her somewhat large mouth, as much variety of

expression when speaking as of strength and sweetness in repose. But the chief character-istic of her handsome face was the eager interest it displayed in anything—whether grave or gay—that moved her, the absence of self-consciousness in her intercourse with both men and women, and the bright smile which was in itself an enchantment. She had great animation of manner, a frank and ringing laugh, and a ready tongue ; all of which were probably calculated to mislead a stranger as to her real character.

"Why are you going to the United States, Miss Ballinger?" again asked Mr. Ferrars.

" The polite answer would be that I am going to see your country, but that would not be quite true," answered the young lady, with a smile. " My brother wished me to come—I am doing so for the sake of being with him."

"You won't like it. Unless you go to the Far West, we have nothing to offer you that you haven't got better in Europe."

" People interest me more than things. One gets wrong ideas of Americans from those one often meets travelling. I shall like studying them on their own soil."

He lit a cigarette before he replied.

"The best types you will probably not see. They do not push themselves prominently forward."

Miss Ballinger's eyes sparkled with amusement.

"One would really think your object was to dissuade me from attempting to see your country."

"My object is to prevent your being disappointed. We are a very young, raw country. Youth, in the educational stage, is apt to offend against good taste. We are made up, at present, of odds and ends. You are sure to get hold of some odds. The ends require to be unravelled."

"I shall try and unravel them."

"Your brother is trying to do so now." He glanced down the row of deck-chairs to where Sir Mordaunt Ballinger sat on a stool, beside the recumbent figure of a lady, so thickly veiled that it was impossible to see if she was young or old. "Have you made Mrs. Courtly's acquaintance? She is rather a complicated skein to unravel."

"We have exchanged a few words—just

enough for me to know that she has a sweet voice and a very gracious manner."

"She is a charming woman, and a clever one. Not that she does anything, or knows anything particularly well, at all events much less than half our highly-educated women. But she has that fine receptive capacity which makes her seize the scope and meaning of most things that do not demand preliminary study. Of course she is called ' superficial,' but what does that mean ? That she has the artistic instinct, unusually developed, in a number of subjects, and an insatiable curiosity about everything."

"I had no idea she was that sort of person— I thought—I had been told that she was very fond of admiration—and—"

" I know all you heard. You need not tell me. She is often misunderstood ; most of all by her own sex. She is fond of dress, and dancing, and admiration. She is religious, and philosophical, and pictorial, and poetical—what is she not in turn ? But she is never ill-natured, never slanderous. A female Proteus."

" You evidently know her well ? "

" I do, but we have always met in Europe.

I have never visited her in New England, where she has a charming house and entertains a great deal."

" Has she been long a widow—for I conclude she is one ? "

" Her husband died several years since, and she has never yet made up her mind to change her state. She had one desperate love affair long ago. Whether it is that has prevented her marrying again, or whether her experience of matrimony was not such as to make her desire to repeat the experiment "—his smile was not pleasant as he said that—" I do not know. I only know she is the best friend in the world, and that women are jealous of her because she attracts all sorts and conditions of men. The lion and the lamb lie down together on her hearth-rug. But she loves the lion better than the lamb."

" Mordaunt is not a lion, neither is he quite a lamb," laughed his sister.

" Oh ! but he will be made a lion of in the States. The son of so eminent a man as your father, whose name was so prominent in our country during the Alabama dispute, will be interviewed, and banqueted, and have receptions given for him, all the time. Most of this you will have to endure also. I hope you won't hate it as much as I should."

" I can't believe that you are right, Mr. Ferrars ; but if greatness is thrust upon me, in this unexpected manner, I hope I shall be amused. I have no idea or *expecting* to be bored with anything. A sense of humour carries one through so much, and I delight in American humour."

" If you expect that everyone is going to talk like Mark Twain, you will be mistaken. You will find a good deal of unconscious humour occasionally in the sayings and doings of my countrymen. I hope it will carry you through those dreary hours—the ladies' luncheons, and all those terrible afflictions ! "

" Must they be afflictions because you are not admitted to them ? " laughed Miss Ballinger.

" Not necessarily. But the tall talk of superior women is bad enough when it has to bend to the level of our comprehension. What it must be when they are alone—"

" Well, they will have to bend to the level of mine. I shall collapse if they ask me, as Miss Lobb did this morning, what influence I considered the ancient religions of Egypt had on the manners and customs of the Western world ? I murmured, ' I suppose it has tended to a love of cats,' and fled."

Ferrars laughed, for the first time. " The old-maid must have taken it as personal. I think, in some prior state of existence, she must have been a cat, though I doubt the Egyptians worshipping her."

" Her voice is very trying. Explain to me why your highly educated people, who talk so much of ' culture,' take so little trouble about training the voice. For the voice *can* be trained, you know."

" Certainly it can, and our singers prove that the American voice is a raw material that can be worked to advantage. But then singing pays, and speaking doesn't."

" Yet you are much given to ' orating ' ! " said Miss Ballinger, with a mischievous twitch of her lips. " Is not every American born to hold forth ? "

" Well ! As the Yankee said, when he stood before Niagara, for the first time, ' What hinders ? ' We are in the rapids of life. Why should the cataract of our impetuosity be

checked ? We have got to do a deal of talking to make leeway and overtake other
nations."

" I think you have overtaken them. Are you
a member of Congress ? "

" Heaven forbid ! What should I do there ? "

" Serve your country, I suppose. You
do not strike me as a good American, Mr.
Ferrars."

" I am too good an American, and too irritable a man, to stand by and see all the job-
bery and corruption that goes on and not raise
my voice. And what good would that do, even
if I were elected, which I doubt ? There are
men shouting their lungs out all the time ; there
are papers, every day, denouncing the acts of a
man like ——, and yet he will continue to be a
member of our administration, until he is hurled
from power, and the Opposition set up *their*
gods in the temple. That is the result of our
beautiful universal suffrage—what you are fast
coming to."

" Are you a Democrat or a Republican ? "

" Who can say what he is, in the present day !
One feels disposed to vote with the Opposition,
whatever it is."

" Perhaps that is your principle through life,"
said Miss Ballinger, demurely, as she bound a
Shetland veil round her face, which the wind
was buffeting too roughly. After that he lost
the sunlight and the cloud-like shadows that
crossed it. The next moment she continued,
" You spoke of the papers just now. If they
denounce corruption, they are not as bad as we
are always told they are."

" Their denunciations lose all weight, because
they vilify everyone. The Angel Gabriel
wouldn't be safe from their attacks. No man's
home, or his most private domestic concerns,
is sacred. No lie is too preposterous for them
to invent, no scandal too hideous for them to
propagate. As no man who brought an action
for libel in the States ever got substantial re-
dress, they carry on their vile trade with impunity, until some editor happens to be shot by
an outraged husband, or father, when the community says complacently : ' Ah, serve him
right ! ' Can you wonder that the best citizens
often shrink from the pillory of election for
office, whether it be the municipal town council
or anything else ? To have their early difficulties, their family griefs (it may be their family

disgrace), their most secret wounds torn open, to be pelted with the rotten eggs of vilification, day after day, what man, unless he be made of adamant, or is sunk so low as to be absolutely indifferent to public opinion, would willingly subject himself to all this?"

" If a man had a very strong sense of public duty, and if his record were a clean one, I should think he would. How are things ever to be improved if all you educated men say this? By-the-bye, what *do* you do with your life, Mr. Ferrars? Something more than vibrate between Europe and America, I suppose?"

" Well, what I do can be done as well on one side of the Atlantic as the other. I was brought up to the study of medicine. But I gave that up when I was still young. Now I do nothing but write."

" Caustic criticism of your own country, I suppose? Anonymous?"

" Yes, anonymous."

" Perhaps you wrote 'Plutocracy,' the authorship of which excited so much curiosity a few years ago?"

" I should not own it if I had," he replied,

rather sharply. " I hold Sir Walter Scott's
line of conduct quite justifiable in such cases.
No secret could be kept if it was necessary to
stand and deliver to the first highwayman who
demanded your treasure."

" So you look on me as a highwayman ! "
laughed the young Englishwoman merrily. " I
assure you, I had no desire to rob you of—"

" You misunderstand me," he interrupted,
looking a little annoyed. " I did not think of
applying the image—a stupid one, I admit—to
you. As a matter of fact, I never write fiction.
What I do write, for personal reasons, I do not
put my name to—and, consequently, consider
myself quite at liberty to repudiate."

The gong sounded for luncheon at this
moment, and Sir Mordaunt rose and came up
to his sister. He was a tall man, with rather too
small a head for his height, but remarkably well-
built, and with that undefinable air of high breeding which is a gift of the gods, bestowed now
and again upon the low-born, but not to be
purchased nor transmitted, depending neither
upon the traditions of Eton, nor the tailoring
of Poole or Johns. He had a frank, intelligent
face, with indications of possible but transient

explosion in the quick flash of the eye and occasional contraction of the brow. But he was more disposed to smile than to scowl through life. His laugh, and his way of speaking, strongly marked by what Americans call " the English accent," resembled his sister's, and there all likeness between them began and ended. Miss Ballinger's personality, to a close observer, conveyed a sense of reserved force under that light manner and readily-responsive smile, which her brother's entirely lacked. As someone expressed it, "All his goods were in his front shop window." There was nothing to be explored, nothing to be connived at, in a nature affectionate if not very profound, pleasure-loving and, as some thought, conceited; quick tempered and, as some thought, occasionally impertinent ; a nature every fold of which was exposed to the light that revealed its spots and the accretions of dust that are apt to gather upon goods that are exposed in front shop windows.

" Come along to luncheon, Grace ! I'm as hungry as a hunter. How do you get on with that Yankee ? I hope he was as entertaining as my widow. She is perfectly charming—I want you to talk to her. She knows almost as much as you do about pictures and things— and she is awfully amusing."

" I have been listening to her praises from Mr. Ferrars, who, by-the-bye, is not a Yankee. He is a Southerner by birth, and a cosmopolitan by choice—an odd man, and clever ; but I don't feel quite sure whether I like him. All the same, I wish his seat at meals was next me. Mr. Gunning, with his narrow little mind centred on himself, is such a bore."

" Mrs. Courtly tells me he is a ' dude,' and tremendously rich. They think no end of him in New York."

" I dare say ; but, as his riches don't interest me, I wish I hadn't to sit next him three times a day for the next week. I had so much rather have that nice old man—Senator something—who looks like a portrait by Tintoret, with his white beard."

" What a queer girl you are ! always cottoning to old men. Gunning is a good-looking chap—talks a little too much about his yacht and his athletics, and his big game ; but I don't think he's half a bad sort."

His sister smiled a subtle, enigmatical smile,

and gently pinched her brother's arm, on which
she leant, as they walked along.

" How well I know you, Mordy! You
wouldn't judge him so leniently if he were a
penniless Englishman, ' something in the City.'
You are at present resolved to see everything
American *en beau*."

" Of course I am. I only wish I had an
American girl with some fun in her next me at
table, instead of that Lady Clydesdale."

" Well! She is American enough, in all
conscience, with her Republican ideas! She
seems to me '*plus royaliste que le roi*,' if one
can use such a Conservative figure of speech
about her."

" Only the fun's wanting. She is in such
deadly earnest, with her rights and her wrongs,
and her emancipation from social slavery, and
all the rest of it."

They had reached the saloon by this time,
and most of the famished passengers were
already seated. Opposite Sir Mordaunt
Ballinger and his sister sat a couple, concerning whom Grace felt a mild curiosity. It had not
been sufficiently strong to prompt her to speak
hitherto, and they were so quiet and retiring,

it was pretty certain they would never take the initiative. Were they husband and wife? Hardly. The lady looked a little older than her companion. She had a sweet, tranquil face, and yet, for all its tranquillity, one read there the lines of suffering and sorrow. Her abundant brown hair was smoothly parted over a brow that was too large for beauty, without fringe or curl, to mitigate the defect in proportion. Her dress was of Puritanic simplicity. She wore no bracelet or ornament of any description, but on her delicate small hand was a wedding-ring.

Her companion, without being ill-built, had the sort of figure which looks as if it had never been trained to athletics, and is unused to active exercise. His hands and feet were almost too small for his height. His chest was contracted; and he had a cough which, without being constant, made itself heard now and again. His smile was a very pleasant one, lighting up the entire face, as some smiles seem incapable of doing; and his rare laugh was merry as a boy's. He wore his clothes badly, and the clothes themselves were ill-made, facts which disqualified him in Sir Mordaunt

Ballinger's estimation, but hardly affected his sister. What did affect her was the curiously intense, powerful young face which rose, beardless, above the loose-tied neckcloth. It was too thin and colourless for manly beauty, though the lines were fine, and the eyes of extraordinary depth. His voice, like his companion's, was low, and except by certain expressions and the pronunciation of certain words, it would not have been apparent that he was American.

On the lady's right sat Mr. Ruggs, from Chicago, who had been to Europe to enlist sympathies for the World's Fair, and who held forth to Lady Clydesdale opposite him as to the wonders of the show, " which I tell you, ma'am, will knock the Paris Exhibition into a cocked hat!" His opulence and prodigality of illustration seemed a little oppressive to the gentlewoman beside him. Her companion had Miss Lobb on his left. That highly-cultured lady tackled him at once upon the subject of undeveloped cosmic forces. Grace asked herself whether he would not be as glad to escape from the cosmic forces as she would be to forego the rapid vehemence of the young man from New York. And so, resolved that the

stream of white cloth should divide her no
longer from her opposite neighbours, she startled
them with this original observation, addressed
indifferently to both,—

"How hungry being at sea makes one!"

The lady responded with a fluttering smile.
"I have not experienced it as yet. I hope my
son will do so soon. He has been sick."

Her son? Grace was astonished. And
sick? Why, the twenty-four hours that had
passed since leaving Liverpool had been absolutely calm. In her expressive countenance
the young man read possibly what was passing
in her mind.

"*You* would say 'ill,'" he observed, with a
smile. "We use the word in the old Scriptural
sense."

"Yes," said his mother, "sick unto death.
He really was that. We have been quite a
time in Europe, in consequence."

"Where were you?" asked Grace. "At
some Baths?"

"Homburg is the only Bath worth going to,"
struck in Mr. Gunning. "Lots going on there
all the time."

"Horrid place! I hate it," said Miss

Bllinger. Then, looking at her opposite neighbour, she continued, " I hope you were at a nice place. How long were you in Europe ? "

" Four months. I was sent right off to Aix-la-Chapelle, after rheumatic fever, and then on to Spa. We had very little time to travel, but we did go around in Belgium and Holland for three weeks."

"One picks up awfully sweet delf and old oak in Holland," said Mr. Gunning.

" What ! You saw nothing of England, then ? And this is your first visit to Europe ? "

Miss Ballinger looked almost indignant as she asked this. The mother answered quickly,—

" It is our first visit, and I never should have come but for my son's health. I should dearly love to visit the cathedral towns, and all the old historical castles in England ; but I guess I never shall."

" Yes, you will," said her son. " I mean to go next fall, and to take you with me. My mother has lived more than twenty-five years in a New England village, without going further than the seashore. She enjoys travel, but she cannot leave home."

"When one has gotten a house and helps, it's difficult to go right away, even if there were no other reason," said the mother, shaking her head. "But *you* can go. There's no call for *you* to spend your vacation at home."

"If one doesn't go to Europe," said Gunning, "the only place is Newport. You must come to Newport, Miss Ballinger—you really must. It's yachting, dancing, or picnics, all the time. You should see how our swells live there. Why, Cowes isn't in it, it isn't really. Our prominent cottagers give such entertainments. Why, there was one luncheon party last year that cost—"

"Don't tell me, Mr. Gunning. It makes me feel that I am a pauper."

Miss Lobb here interposed to observe that it was only in effete old countries that pauperism was tolerated. She looked through her double glasses defiantly at Grace as she added, "With us it is exterminated."

Sir Mordaunt Ballinger's face was convulsed with suppressed laughter, as he touched his sister's elbow at this moment. "Listen to Mr. Ruggs' account of Chicago. If it doesn't make you wish to go there! Will you tell my sister what you were saying about your city ? "

"I tell you, miss," said the fat little man, turning a pair of twinkling eyes on Grace, and with an expression so shrewd and humorous that she felt uncertain how far he was in earnest, how far endeavouring to impose on her credulity, "I tell you, miss, we are going to have the finest city in the whole creation. Don't you make a mistake. There will be nothing to touch it, until the New Jerusalem is built. Why, already it takes more than two hours to drive from one end of it to the other! We've got a street twelve miles long. We've got a tonsorial saloon paved with dollar pieces, and a hotel of alabaster and gold. I tell you, miss, there is nothing to touch it in Europe!"

"And about the World's Fair, Mr. Ruggs—tell us what you propose doing," asked Sir Mordaunt.

"Well, sir, we propose bringing over a few of your European princes, and having them on show. We are in treaty for the Duke of Braganza, as direct descendant of Columbus, whose bones we feel like having if we can, but, odd to say, they make some difficulties. The

bones and the descendants will come right over
in galleons made on the model of those that
brought Columbus. We also propose to bring
over the Sphinx—"

"What! From Egypt?" Miss Ballinger
laughed outright. "Poor Sphinx! It will feel
very strange away from its native desert."

"Oh! we'll blow a lot of sand up right around
it. We've got plenty on the shore of our lake.
That's for the classical advertisement. Then,
for the Scriptural one, I did think of
having Pharaoh in the Red Sea, and dividing
the water by hydraulic pressure; but making
the waves red might create a sort of a feeling
—the citizens might feel kinder uncomfortable.
There's no reason against the Garden of Eden;
plenty of apple-trees and snakes are common;
there's only a little difficulty about Adam and
Eve. However, I've no doubt we shall
hit on something. People do like something
Scriptural. There's Ammergau, now! That
would do fust-rate, only those peasants wouldn't
come."

"But you're going to have a bigger theatre
than the world has ever seen, I suppose?"

"We have one, sir, and as to acting, have

you seen our Clara Morris? I tell you, sir, there is nothing in creation like it! Why, when she weeps on the stage, it is enough to make an iron dog come down from a door-step and lick her hand! Don't talk to me of your Burnhards, and your Ristor-*eyes*. Not but what we'll have them too, just to show how superior the *reel* American article is!"

"And pictures—are you going in for pictures?"

"I believe you, sir! Why, the pictures at the Paris Exhibition 'll be like a pack of playing cards, compared with ours. I calculate we'll have the biggest picture on show that has ever been seen. It's forty-two feet long. I've concluded to bid half price for it, when our show is over, and to present it to the city."

Here Lady Clydesdale, who was on the other side of Sir Mordaunt, struck in her oar, and a powerful one it was. She was what Mr. Ruggs styled "a fine female, but fleshy," and her arrogant assumption of humility was irritating to others besides the young baronet; perhaps, to none more than to Americans.

"I am sorry to hear you say," she observed

quickly, and in a voice like a trumpet, " that you are going to imitate the follies of Europe, in attaching any importance, or giving any prominence, to princes. It is degrading to distinguish one individual above another, except for personal merit."

" Yours and mine are beyond question, Lady Clydesdale," laughed Ballinger, parenthetically.

It was impertinent ; but he was nettled. She turned and rent him.

" My principles and practice are too well-known at home for me to argue with you, Sir Mordaunt. I would resign my coronet to-morrow. I would abolish all class distinctions. I would herd with the humblest. I would dine with my servants, and give them all the luxuries I enjoy myself—the piano, horses, carriages— they should live as I do did the prejudices of society permit it. I expected to find it more enlightened in America than in England. I thought there was one country, at least, where all men were equal ! I am disappointed."

What Mr. Ruggs' rejoinder was, for he did rejoin, and how the battle was fought, Miss Ballinger never heard, for Gunning, who had been listening to her ladyship's onslaught in amazement, here said in an undertone,—

" Is she mad ? Fancied we were all equal ! Why, we are just as exclusive as ever we can be in New York. The Four Hundred shut their doors against everyone who hasn't money, I can tell you."

" Ah ! brains count for nothing, I suppose."

" Nothing out of Wall Street. A man must work, of course, to make his pile, if he doesn't inherit one. I was an only child. Lucky, wasn't I ? Never had to work."

" Those who have to work are the lucky ones, in my opinion."

He looked surprised, and shook his head.

"Couldn't have my yacht, or my team— couldn't go off to shoot in the Rockies— couldn't do lots of things, if I had to work. Then getting up early every morning—oh, it wouldn't suit me ! " After a minute's pause, he went on, " You'll let me drive you in my team one day ? I'll get up a luncheon party for you somewhere in the country. We'll have a band and dance afterwards. We'll have a rare good time."

" I shall do whatever my brother likes in New

York. You must ask him. I shall have absolutely no will of my own. Will you give me
those biscuits ? Thank you."

"We call them crackers. About your brother,
I'll see that we have a lot of bright girls.
There's Miss Planter; she is a belle, she will
just suit him. She was made a lot of in
London last season, I believe. She will have
a million of dollars. Not bad, eh ? "

" Bad, if she is to be married for the sake of
them. It is fortunate she is attractive. I am
glad that I have only enough to keep body
and soul alive. No one will marry *me* for my
money."

"Oh, well, it won't signify to you having
nothing—" he stopped short, and smiled at her.
Then, though the connection of ideas was not
very clear, he went on, " I say, Miss Ballinger,
this is the second time I have been to Europe,
but I've never seen anything of English society.
I have fooled around in Paris and London a
bit, but I have a mind next year to take a place
in England and hunt. Do you think I should
like it ? They say Englishwomen don't take
to American men ; is that so ? "

" We know so few ; most of you are too absorbed in business to spend much time with us, but your women are very popular. My brother says they are so much easier to get on with than his own countrywomen."

"That's right enough, but are not we American men easy to get on with as well?"

"Certainly; perhaps too easy sometimes. But, having got on, the thing is to remain on. I have heard it complained sometimes that Americans lose ground by assurance. If you come to England, I dare say you will be made a great deal of because you are a rich young man. But if you want to be popular with anyone besides manœuvring mammas, take my advice—never talk about your money, never presume upon it in any way; the nicest people resent that. I am going on deck; it is so hot here."

She delivered herself of this little homily simply, almost laughingly, and rose, leaving the young man to his half-finished luncheon. The mother opposite, without waiting for her son, upon whom Miss Lobb had once again fastened her fangs, had risen from the table, and Miss Ballinger followed and joined her on deck.

CHAPTER II.

" MAY I walk up and down with you ? " (The gentle little woman smiled her assent.) " I was never more surprised than to hear you were the mother of the young man opposite me. You look like his eldest sister."

" I was married very young."

" Is he your only child ? "

" The only one alive. I lost two younger. That is why I—why we are doubly anxious about him."

"Your husband is alive, then ? What is he ? "

It was only this young woman's great charm of manner which prevented her curiosity sometimes from seeming obtrusive. But there was such genuine interest in the look of her clear, truthful eyes, that no one, least of all the gentle unsophisticated creature she addressed, could resent it.

" My husband is a minister. Our name is

Barham. We live in a very quiet village in
New England, and seldom leave it. Of course,
I should not have gone abroad with Saul had
it not been for his health. But my husband
urged it, and so I went."

"And you are glad you went, I am sure.
As you were anxious about your son, it must
have been a great comfort to you to be with
him. Has he always been delicate?"

"Well, he has never been very strong."
Here she sighed. "We feared lung trouble at
one time. Our climate is rather trying, and
Saul overworked himself."

"Was he at Harvard University? I am
sure he is very clever."

"Yes, he is very clever. When he left
Harvard, he became a teacher. Then they
made him a professor at the University a few
months ago—a great compliment to so young
a man. But whether his health will stand it—"
Here she sighed again, and left her sentence
unfinished.

"But he is going now to return to his
work?"

"Why, certainly. He would not give that
up for the world. He was offered a fine salary

to remain in Europe and travel with two boys.
It would have been a grand thing for his health,
and he would have made more money than he
can do at home, but he would not accept it.
He has a deal of ambition, you see, and there's
—there's something else—he is so fond of me,
he couldn't bear to leave me and go right
away. Here he comes; don't say anything to
him about his health, Miss—"

"Miss Ballinger. No, I will not. I am so
much obliged to you for telling me so much
about yourselves. Mr. Barham, I am going to
introduce myself formally to you. Your mother
and I have been making friends. It is like
being at a masquerade, not knowing who and
what people are, and it saves so much idle
speculation and back-stair ferreting out, to
label oneself at once. I am Miss Ballinger,
spinster, aged twenty-five, travelling with her
brother, Sir Mordaunt Ballinger, Baronet and
Member of Parliament. Any discreet question
you like to ask I am prepared to answer, for I
have a mania for asking questions myself, as
your mother knows by this time, and I don't
want any unfair advantage."

The young man looked at her fixedly for a

moment, and then laughed. He had never met anyone like this young lady. Was she a specimen of her country? He knew so few of them.

"All the questions I shall ask will be mental ones, which you will answer whether you like it or not," he said. "I find these replies, unconsciously given, so much more satisfying than any others. Little mother, you look tired; lie down here. Perhaps Miss Ballinger will continue her quarter-deck walk with me."

He tucked up the "little mother" on a deck-chair with a plaid round her legs; then turned and resumed his walk with Miss Ballinger.

She began at once, "What a charming face Mrs. Barham has! She' reminds me of Scheffer's picture of the mother of St. Augustine, only younger."

"Yes. It is a pity I am not more like him. The only point of resemblance that I can recall is that, whenever I pray to be made good, I add, like Augustine, 'but not to-day, O Lord!'"

She turned her bright, penetrating glance full upon him, half-laughing, half-serious.

"Are you one of the men who are anxious to

be thought very wicked ? I should not have expected that. But there I am, questioning again ! Well, never mind. Strong characters are rarely saints in youth, I suppose, though I don't know why they shouldn't be—if they are only strong *enough*."

" Perhaps I am not strong at all."

" Yes, you are. Your mouth and chin told me that before you spoke."

" You are a physiognomist. How about the eyes ? Do you attach any importance to them, those ' windows of the soul ' ? "

" He does not expect me to say that his windows are luminous ones, magnificently draped, does he ? If he does, he shall be disappointed," thought Grace. What she said was, " Eyes are the most deceptive feature. There is no trusting them. I have grown quite tired of fine eyes."

The young American smiled in a peculiar manner. " I am beginning my mental questions."

" What do you mean ? "

" I am wondering whether you yourself are always as perfectly truthful."

She flushed and looked annoyed. " You

are quite justified. Of course I was not speaking the exact truth, though it is really my opinion that eyes do not denote character."

"I think your eyes do—better than your words, perhaps."

"As how?"

He smiled again. "Well, that brings the confession that *I* was not perfectly truthful. I was not wondering; I never doubted that you were truthful, and straightforward —generally, though you might say things that were not quite so, sometimes."

She burst out laughing.

"Upon my word, Mr. Barham! That is a pretty character, and unfortunately, it is quite true. It is lucky I am not like Mrs. Van Winkle—have you spoken to Mrs. Van Winkle? She is most amusing—who told me she loved flattery, in every form—there was no amount of it she could not swallow! Now, I like it, of course—what woman doesn't? But it must be in homœopathic doses. You have administered an infinitesimal grain of it wrapped up in a very wholesome bitter. I shall take care what I say to you in future."

" Pray don't.   That would be punishing my impertinence too severely.   Yes, Mrs. Van Winkle spoke to me this morning, hearing I was from Harvard.   She said she felt that those who were fellow-workers in one field should interchange thoughts.   I suppose I stared, for she hastened to inform me that she had written a book which was pronounced to be a work of genius."

" Her *naïveté* is quite delightful ! "

" Presently she went on to tell me that a painter had begged her to sit to him as Clio, when she was in Rome, and that her hands and feet had been modelled by a sculptor in Paris. I suppose that was *naïve.*"

" Certainly, it was.   Most of us would have gone a roundabout way to convey the same information.   We are all vain.   My vanity is fed by the belief that people will find out what a nice person I am, without my giving a sort of auctioneer's inventory of my merits, as that dear innocent Mrs. Van Winkle does."

" Innocent ?   Well, she told me her husband would be the next Minister to England, and that she would not return there till then, as she did not choose to go about having to explain herself. I thought—with the Paris sculptor and the modelling—that a *foot*-note might be explanation enough. But I have not an idea what she meant."

"She meant that the Van Winkles are not to be herded with common travelling Americans."

"I have been a common travelling American myself for the last three months."

"And I daresay you *had* sometimes to explain yourself."

"Never. I know too well the way in which my pushing countrymen are spoken of, to seek anyone. Those who have sought me have had to do so without any 'explanation.'"

"Proud as Lucifer," thought Grace. "Clearly *not* the stuff of which saints are made." Then aloud, "How did you like Europe?"

"Very much, for a time—for many times, I might say. I should like to travel there yearly. I hope it may be possible for me to do so. But I would not live out of my own country."

"Because you prefer it as a residence, or from a sense of duty?"

He demurred. " The associations of early
life have a strong hold on one, and there are
special reasons in my case, why—" Here he
broke off, then began anew, " Of course there
are things I dislike, things I deplore, in my
own country, but she has a great future before
her, and it behoves every American to do his
best to advance that future, so that the genera-
tion that follows may be richer than the
present in wisdom and in worth."

" Not only in wealth ? "

" You have been told that is the only god we
worship ? Well, that is true, perhaps, of the
majority ; not of all. And this god, when he
has been won by the self-made man, is generally
a very munificent god with us. Where will
you find colleges, hospitals, libraries, galleries,
the gift of private individuals, to the same
extent as with us ? Every city has its record
of them—a record to be proud of."

" I see I shall have to strike a balance in my
judgments between you and Mr. Ferrars. He
is pessimist, and you are optimist, as regards
your country."

" I do not know Mr. Ferrars," said the young
man, drily. " But it is a cheap way of showing

your superiority, to decry your own nation and point out all its shortcomings."

"There is such a thing as exaggerated patriotism that will not admit shortcomings. As a nation, you are so over-sensitive to criticism. Why, you will not allow one of your own best writers to represent certain types, to laugh at certain follies, without crying out that he is unpatriotic! The whole stock-in-trade of Dickens and Thackeray was laughing at our shams and vulgarities, and who ever thought of bringing such a charge against *them*?"

"We *are* over-sensitive, but then we are very young, remember."

Here a slight accident interrupted their progress. Mrs. Courtly was emerging from the main gangway just as Miss Ballinger and her companion crossed it, and a lurch of the vessel, for the wind had been gradually rising and the sea was no longer perfectly smooth, sent the unprepared lady, adroit and nimble as she was, into the young man's arms. She was a small, slight woman, exquisitely built and proportioned, no longer in her first youth, with a pale face lit by a wonderful smile, which

recalled to Grace Leonardo da Vinci's enigmatical " Joconde."

Apologies on both sides, with a good deal
of laughing on the lady's part, followed.
Grace came forward, and a few words were
exchanged, during which Barham took off his
hat and walked away, to Miss Ballinger's
surprise—perhaps, it may be said, to her annoy-
ance.

"Who is your friend whom I so unceremoni-
ously embraced ? " asked Mrs. Courtly, in her
low, musical voice. " Why is he gone away ?
I am so sorry to have interrupted your walk."

" If he had wished, I suppose, he would
have stayed. He is a professor from Harvard
University ; his name is Barham."

" Really ? I never heard of him, and I
have so many friends at Harvard. My home
in Massachusetts is not so very far distant.
He is very good-looking ; is he clever ? "

" Certainly ; but not much of a society-man.
He suffers from a form of shyness which I
suppose is not common in the States—a dread
of being thought forward, pushing. I am sure
that is why he beat a retreat."

" How very singular ! It was I who was

forward and pushing!" Here she laughed softly. "You must present him formally to me; I shall be delighted to make his acquaintance; I love to gather round me all that is best worth knowing. By the way, your brother has been promising to bring you to stay with me. I am within easy reach of Boston; I hope you won't object."

"You are very good; it sounds delightful. I have always looked forward to seeing Boston, and I hope my brother will go there. I have heard there is nothing like Boston society."

"You must not expect the magnificence of New York. We New Englanders live much more simply; but there is a pleasant mixture of the grave and the gay. I am reproached with being too gay—too frivolous for my years. But my principle is to enjoy everything as long as I can, to live and to let live. And so I get a great deal of pleasure out of existence."

She said this in a low, cooing voice that was wonderfully persuasive.

"And confer a great deal," rejoined Grace. "Most people get so soon *blasés*, it is refreshing to find anyone who retains youthfulness of spirit into middle age. But, then, you have a

wonderful variety of interests in life, I am
told."

"Oh, yes; I care for a great many things, I
am glad to say—books, and pictures, and
people. If I cannot get some excitement out
of one, I do out of another; life is so curious,
so full of problems. Who told you about me?
If you listen to all you hear—"

"It was Mr. Ferrars—evidently a very true
friend—who spoke of you."

"Oh! poor Quintin Ferrars! Yes, he is a
good friend."

"Why do you say 'poor'?"

"Because he has not had a happy life."

"Partly his own fault, I should think. He
strikes me as not having a happy temperament."

"Is that his own fault?" asked Mrs.
Courtly, smiling. "He has not a happy temperament, it is true. I have always told him
that he does not extract the enjoyment he
might out of life—though it struck me he was
doing so successfully this morning! But, poor
fellow, he has been heavily handicapped; circumstances have been against him, they have
embittered everything."

Grace was dying to ask what those circumstances were, but something restrained her. Her acquaintance with Mrs. Courtly was but slight; it would hardly be seemly for Grace to press for information about Mrs. Courtly's friend which that lady thought fit to conceal. Presently Mrs. Courtly said,—

"Will you come and have tea in my cabin at five o'clock? I have a deck cabin; it can hold half-a-dozen people—Mrs. Van Winkle, and your brother, and Quintin Ferrars, and one other man; shall I ask Jem Gunning?"

"Not for me, please, I have enough of him at three meals every day. Do you like him?"

"Why, yes. Jem is not a bad boy in his way. A clever woman would twist Jem round her finger, and might make him very different to what he is."

"What he is, is not pleasing to me at present. Perhaps if I meet him hereafter, when he has been duly twisted by the clever woman, I may appreciate him more."

"How sarcastic you are!" purred Mrs. Courtly, showing her white teeth; "all our young men will be quite afraid of you, Miss Ballinger."

" I am not sarcastic—far from it," said Grace,
laughing.   " Only I know what I like and what
I don't."

"You prefer your friend, the Harvard Professor ? "   She smiled with a malicious twinkle
in her hazel eyes.   " Well, will you invite him ?
Bring him with you."

Grace was a little taken aback.   " I—I can't
bring him.   I will deliver your message . . .
if I see him . . .   But he is no *friend* of mine.
I never spoke to him till half an hour ago."

After a few more words interchanged, the
two ladies separated.   Later in the afternoon,
Grace found Mr. Barham, seated by his mother
reading, in the upper deck cabin.   It had by
this time become rough and cold, and only the
very hardy were still pacing the deck.

" I have a message from Mrs. Courtly (the
lady who would have fallen but for you to-day).
She wishes to make your acquaintance, Mr.
Barham, and asks if you will come and have
tea in her cabin at five o'clock.   My brother
and I are going."

The young man had laid down his book, and
had risen.   He looked much surprised.

" What can Mrs. Courtly—want to know me

for ? I am not a society man, and I cannot do anything to amuse her . . . But . . . of course . . . if . . . you are quite sure—"

"I should not transmit such a message if I were not quite sure. You will do as you please about accepting the invitation." Then, turning abruptly to Mrs. Barham, " Can you recommend to me a thoroughly representative American book ? I mean representative of real American life, not from the satirical, or humorist point of view. I see there is a capital library here."

"Our New-England life is very well depicted in Mary Wilkins' tales, and also in Sarah Orne Jewett's. They are truthful pictures of our quiet homes, or quiet lives removed from the turmoil of the great cities. But perhaps you might find them dull."

"I have read them, and thought them charming. Spinsterhood is great, and Miss Wilkins is its prophet. But I want to know about something besides those dear old women. Miss Jewett, also, charming as she is, is circumscribed. I want something wider in range. I was given ' On Both Sides ' the other day. It amused me, but as a caricature."

"You mean that the English are caricatured —not the American," said Saul Barham with a smile.

"Yes, I do. No woman in society ever said the outrageously vulgar things Mrs. Sykes is made to say. She may *think* them—she may even act them—she could not *say* them. It strikes a false note. Then there is a beautiful young man, supposed to be a typical young man of society, who tells a long story in which he repeats over and over again, ' I *says* to him.' Why! no one above a stable-boy ever used such a form of speech."

"Is it quite possible for one nation to judge another fairly?" asked Mrs. Barham gently.

"I hope so. Why not? I am sure I have no anti-American prejudices. But as we are so closely bound together by language and origin, it is more difficult for us not to look at differences between us from an English stand-point, than it is when we are discussing any European nation. And no doubt it is the same with you, if you confess it."

"I do confess it," said the young man.

Mrs. Barham murmured something about there being "quite a number of persons in

America who imitate everything English now."

Saul laughed.

" Why, we have a cousin who is so anxious to be taken for an Englishman, that we can scarcely understand what he says, he swallows his words so."

After which he recommended two books to Grace, one of which she found on the shelves disengaged, and departed with it.

CHAPTER III.

THE small gathering in Mrs. Courtly's cabin at five o'clock, which looked at first as if it would be what Mordaunt Ballinger called " frosty," ended, by reason of the hostess's tact and charm of manner, in assimilating fairly well. The men were of course the difficult ingredients to " mix ; " they always are, when not homogeneous. Ballinger felt, and rightly, that he and Ferrars had not much in common ; it would require a shipwreck to make them intimate. Ferrars probably did not trouble his head about the young baronet, except as being the brother of the most delightful girl he thought he had ever met. Saul Barham was an unknown quantity to both men ; to Ballinger he was "a young Yankee, not bad-looking, but a willowy sort of chap, got up in a reach-me-down, and wants his hair cut awfully." Ferrars regarded his young countryman superciliously, as he did most things at first. And the young Harvard Professor showed no keen desire to conciliate either of the men, whom he now spoke to for the first time. Mrs. Van Winkle displayed an evident intention of securing Sir Mordaunt Ballinger's undivided attention, by inviting him to share a portmanteau with her, the seats in the cabin being few. But it was not to indulge in *têtes-à-têtes* that Mrs Courtly had brought her friends together; they could do that on deck. With the pouring out of the Russian tea, and the diffusion of some wonderful cakes, produced from a tin, she contrived adroitly to break up the duets, for Ferrars was talking art in a low voice to Miss Ballinger, and she herself had been drawing out the young Professor. She felt that the conversation ought now to become general.

"You must come and see me when you are back in Cambridge," she had been saying to Barham, as she made tea. "I am quite an easy distance by rail from there, and I want you to look over my books. I am devoted to books . . . not that I am a great scholar, far from it. Do you read Italian? Yes! I am so glad.

Then, with your knowledge of Latin, you will help me to decipher some old provincial poems which I picked up at Quarritchs' the other day, an d of which I believe there are very few copies extant. I have some Elzevirs, too, that may interest you, and several first editions. Talking of first editions, dear Miss Van Winkle, is it true that the whole of the first edition of your 'Phryne' is sold out? Have you read it, Sir Mordaunt? Of course *you* have, Quintin!"

The men were spared replying, by the fair authoress, a decorative woman, with lively eyes, and a very elaborate pink tea gown.

"The demand for my book has been very great," she said, with a sweet smile, "but I know nothing of the details. I have had applications from all the chief magazines begging me to write for them, and I suppose I must do so. Of course my name has something to do with the success. People know that, as a leader of society, I write of what I understand."

"Then I conclude your book is modern, and has nothing to do with the famous Greek . . . beauty?" inquired Ferrars gravely.

" Only by analogy," replied Mrs. Van Winkle, sipping her tea slowly. " The whole world sits in judgment now upon any woman whose beauty or whose talent makes her conspicuous. If she has a symmetrical form, she is always accused of being too *decolletée*."

"You forget that the judges forgave Phryne."

"Oh! they were *men*. Of course it isn't men's tongues a woman has to fear in society. They will make love to her, and praise her before and behind her back, if she amuses them —and encourages them just a little. It is the wives and the mothers, *they* are the Areopagus which sits in judgment upon the woman who attracts men."

"You must have suffered severely at their hands," said Sir Mordaunt as he looked up into her face, with an amused expression.

" I don't know about *suffered*. We are all arraigned, we married women, who amuse ourselves, and who have inspired perhaps a *grande passion;* is it not true, Mrs. Courtly? But they are a little afraid of *me*. When a gifted woman has social position, and fortune, she is comparatively safe. She may follow her

own course, and is only accused of the eccen-
tricities of genius—or, at worst, of being a little
mad. "I know," she added, complacently, as
she bit a cake with her small white teeth, "that
is what they say of me."

Mrs. Courtly felt rather uncomfortable at the
turn the conversation had taken. She was
not quite sure how far Miss Ballinger might be
amused or be scared by Mrs. Van Winkle's
utterances. It was necessary to make a diversion, before one of the men should throw back
the ball ; so she said quickly,—

"Isn't it Marcus Aurelius—or somebody—
who says, ' It is a good thing to be abused ' ?
And, as you say, your position is so well established! You will look after Miss Ballinger and
her brother in New York, I know, and see that
they get invitations to anything that is going
on. How long do you remain there, Miss
Ballinger ? "

"You must ask my brother. He has some
business in New York. The length of our stay
depends entirely on him."

"I shall do all that lies in my power to make
it agreeable to you," said Mrs. Van Winkle,
with cordiality. Her glance, which was at first

directed to Grace, revolved slowly, till it rested on Sir Mordaunt.

"I am glad to hear you have business," said Ferrars, addressing the latter directly, for the first time. "With an object—a direct interest —your visit to the United States may repay you. I was telling Miss Ballinger that if she expected either picturesque beauty or art, she would be disappointed, but she declares, like Pope, that "the proper study of mankind is man," and she comes among us, wishing to see something of our society. You will show her the most costly samples of our social fabrics, Mrs. Van Winkle, but how about brains? You who are such a decorative ornament of literature, I hope you will get together some clever people for Miss Ballinger."

"Oh! brains are of no account in our New York society. I might pick up a brain or two, if I were to sweep around very diligently, per- haps, but the world I live in is intensely frivo- lous, and whenever I meet a clever man, I feel like putting him under a glass case, he's too good for daily use. Miss Ballinger will have to get Mr. Barham to show her the brains of society at Cambridge."

Here she smiled sweetly at the young man ;
and he spoke for the first time, laughing lightly,
as he said,—

" I am afraid we are all in glass cases there,
classified and catalogued.   But without putting
Mrs. Van Winkle to the labour of searching for
brains in New York, I am sure if Miss Ballinger meets some of our brilliant lawyers and
noted speakers, she will find there is as good
talk to be listened to there as anywhere in
Europe.   I hope she will not judge of American
society from any one set, or any single specimen."

"Quite right, Mr. Barham," said Mrs.
Courtly, with a kindly nod.   "Though hardly
complimentary to *us*, I think you are quite
right.   No Frenchman would have said that ;
but you are too much in earnest, to think of our
feelings, Mrs. Van Winkle's, and mine."

Miss Ballinger came to his defence.   " It is
really more complimentary to think you both
incapable of personally applying Mr. Barham's
remark than if he had fenced it round with
those leafless twigs of conventional politeness
which only draw attention to what they were
meant to conceal."

"The leaves, themselves, did that in Paradise," murmured Mrs. Van Winkle, leaning back with a dreamy air.

Ballinger was the only one who laughed. Mrs. Courtly coughed, and did not seem quite at ease. Ferrars said quickly,—

"Mr. Barham is quite right. Nothing is so misleading as personal experience in forming our estimate of a nation. My friend goes to England, and lives in his hotel all the time (and very bad hotels they often are, it must be owned), I have the good chance to meet a few people I know, and am received with kindness and hospitality. What are our respective opinions worth? Never generalize from in-dividuals. Out of us four Americans who are round this table, only Mr. Barham, perhaps, is the least a typical product of our country."

"Why so?" asked Miss Ballinger.

"Because I see he has great belief in our institutions, our future, our indomitable force. As to me, I gave up any such belief when I was twenty. You said yesterday you doubted if I was a good American. If to believe that our crooked paths are straight, our rough ways smooth, and to proclaim on the housetops that

we are the greatest nation on earth—if this is
to be a good American, then I am not one."

"I never heard that to love one's country
was to be blind to her faults," said Barham,
quickly.

"Mr. Ferrars belongs to no country," Mrs.
Van Winkle fanned herself as she spoke, with
half-closed eyes. "Nor do I. I am more
like a Russian, I believe—a Russian George
Sand—that is what I feel like. And you, dear
Mrs. Courtly? Are you not more French?
Madame Recamier, with any number of
Chateaubriands round you, it suits you to a
T."

"Are Chateaubriands so plentiful?" laughed
Mrs. Courtly gently. "I wish I could find
them! They would last so long, too. Madame
Recamier's friendships did not depend upon
her youth. I should like to end my days lying
on a sofa, and surrounded by my old friends."

"Nothing reconciles one so much to the
trouble of living as those strong links which
stand the test of time," said Ferrars, looking
with steady, level eyes at Mrs. Courtly.

"Ah! Quintin, yours is one of those iron
natures whose links never melt—not very

malleable, but which will stand any amount of strain, as I know."

" Never melts ? " exclaimed Mrs. Van Winkle, opening her pretty blue eyes, in affected wonder. " I prefer a man who melts."

" And whose links are of gold ? " said Ferrars, without looking at her. Then he went on, while a flush mounted to her cheek, " I am not one of the precious metals."

" There is a great deal of brass," replied the lady, more tartly than she had yet spoken. " Give me another cup of tea, dear, with lots of sugar, I want something sweet after Mr. Ferrars' acidity. So you are going to the Far West, your brother tells me, Miss Ballinger ? What a journey ! "

" And yet you think nothing of running backwards and forwards to Europe ? " laughed Grace.

" Oh ! traversing our own continent is different ; not half such a change, and very trying to the complexion. Even in the East, one gets awfully dried up. Then, there is nothing to see when one gets there."

" It is not only prophets who have no honour in their own country ! " cried Sir Mordaunt.

" Fancy, my sister has never seen the Tower of London ! and it is the more shameful as I was there for a year."

"Not imprisoned?" inquired Mrs. Van Winkle, with mock gravity.

" The next thing to it—I was quartered there."

" Then you are a guardsman? I always wondered whether all guardsmen were like Guy Livingston. Now I know."

" Well, you see in me a deceased guardsman. I left the service a few months ago."

" Do tell me what brings you out to America ? An heiress ? Of course, you have been very wicked. Are you going to ' *ranger* ' yourself ? "

" Neither reformation nor matrimony is in my mind, I am afraid," laughed Ballinger. " Only self-interest and curiosity. I have one or two friends—one, a brother-officer settled on a ranche in Colorado. I am going to look about and see if I can find a good investment for a little money."

" I think it will be so refreshing to see ranche-life, after the conventionalities of civilization," said Grace.

" You will find a week of it will go a long

way," and Mrs. Courtly shook her head. To her, existence, without its intellectual refinements and pictorial luxuries—all the delicate and varied *entrées* she provided for herself in the pleasant feast which she called " life "—without these, existence would hardly be worth having.

" I would rather live on a ranche than work in Wall Street all my days,' said Barham.

" Wall Street has solid compensations," observed Ferrars.

" I think money can be too dearly bought," returned the younger man quickly. " At the sacrifice of all independence, I would not be rich, if I could."

" How sweet of you, Mr. Barham ! In these mercenary days to hear such a sentiment from a man, it is quite too lovely for anything ! "

Mrs. Van Winkle spoke the words with a languid drawl, but there was a humorous twinkle in her eye. In point of fact, it was often difficult to tell how far she meant her utterances to be taken seriously. Grace, in the spirit of anti-humbug struck in gaily,—

" I am a Philistine. I like riches. I should like to know once how it feels to be *very* rich. I think I could work in Wall Street—whatever

that may mean—all my life if I could earn lots
of money ; but I never shall."

Barham looked at her with a steady gaze.
Was she in earnest ?

" I heard the worship of wealth was as great
in London as in New York—but I did not
believe it."

" Well," said Mordaunt, "all I can say is, I
know several instances in the Life Guards where
a fellow's having a pot of money prejudiced
other fellows against him.   They sent him to
Coventry, because his father dropped his h's,
and they made up their mind the son couldn't
be a gentleman.   I know one very nice chap
who couldn't stand it—had to leave.   So you
see the worship of money isn't universal."

"We don't drop our h's," Ferrars said.
" But there are few colloquial sins we may not
commit with impunity, if we have half a million
of dollars a year, and entertain."

" Ah !   You have it there ! " interposed Mrs.
Van Winkle.   " Our rich people are bound to
entertain.   Otherwise they are of no account.
It is very logical.   We, of the blue blood, want
amusements, but are too poor to give magnificent fêtes.   We honour them with our

presence, and the obligation is more than repaid."

"And I honour the sentiment. It is worthy of blue blood, and it carries conviction with it."

" Mr. Ferrars is detestably satirical, but no one minds what he says," and the lady rose. " It is nearly dinner time. We must leave you, my dear." And so the party broke up.

Next day Mrs. Courtly found an opportunity of saying to Miss Ballinger, in her soft, deprecatory way,—

" I am afraid you may form a false impression of Mrs. Van Winkle. She is really a very kind woman, as well as a clever one, and she is a very good wife, too, only you see her failings. She likes to astonish people. That makes her say things occasionally which— which she had better not."

Grace smiled. " I suppose she has been spoilt, she gives one that idea. Did she marry for money ? "

" Why, no ! What made you think that ? "

" She looked so annoyed when Mr. Ferrars talked of ' links of gold." I am sure he meant something disagreeable by it. He looked it."

"Mr. Van Winkle is by no means rich, but she married him because she was in love: and they are really very happy. He is of a very good old Knickerbocker family. She is very proud of that, as you see. She has always a train of admirers; it means nothing: and Mr. Van Winkle does not object. That is to say, he doesn't *generally*. It is said he did so once, in the case of a man who was very rich, when some one ill-naturedly started the idea that this person helped the establishment along. It got to Mr. Van Winkle's ears, and he gave the man his *congé* there and then. It is the only time he ever asserted his authority, and I am not sure that his wife did not like him all the better for it. If Quintin Ferrars meant anything by his 'golden links,' it was that; but I really think it was a chance shot, and Mrs. Van Winkle—"

"What about her?" said Sir Mordaunt. He had come up, unperceived by Mrs. Courtly; and she stopped short on seeing him. "I think that woman is the greatest sport I've met, for a week of Sundays! How she does blow her own trumpet! I never can be dull in New York as long as she is there. What sort of fellow is the male Winkle, Mrs. Courtly ? "

" A very nice man, but he doesn't amount to much. He is a *Van.* You mustn't call him Winkle—*tout court.*"

" A descendant of the famous Rip, I suppose. We have all had rips for ancestors, at some time or other, no doubt ! " and the young man laughed.

" For shame ! to decry your pedigree in that way ! We are very proud of our descent, when we have any ; and if we know who our great-grandfather was, we always speak of him as having fought in the War of Independence."

The brother and sister laughed ; and the subject of the Van Winkles was not continued further.

CHAPTER IV.

The rest of the voyage was performed swiftly, and uneventfully. Mordaunt Ballinger walked the quarter-deck for hours with certain American men, whom he encouraged to talk of their various interests and enterprises, and believed he was gaining a vast store of useful information thereby. The acquaintances brought together in Mrs. Courtly's cabin saw more or less of each other, according to their proclivities : and in some cases intimacies were formed which could hardly die the natural death which is the common lot of close companionship on board ship. This was especially so in the friendship which Miss Ballinger had established with the Barhams, and though they lay more out of her path, so to speak, than the others, she resolved not to let the threads of her intercourse with mother and son drop, on landing. She felt really interested in the young man : she should be sorry to think this was to be the end of their long talks and discussions, pacing the deck, or watching the moonlight upon the sea, on warm nights, as they leant over the bulwarks.

Quintin Ferrars also she had grown to know, and to like better. That is to say, she liked some parts of him better, and disliked other parts less: recognized his ability, and made more allowances for his cynicism ; as all women do for the cynicism of a man who is never cynical at their expense. Conversation with him stimulated thought : and, though it generally roused opposition, left something behind it, to be pondered over and rediscussed with that other self, which only makes itself heard very often when both speakers are silent.

Mrs. Courtly, Grace admired and liked more and more. She had expected to find the gracious little lady too much of "a man's woman " to take much thought for her, an English girl. They could have but a small community of interest, she thought; and "men's women " were, as a rule, distasteful to her. But, whatever her faults might be, Mrs.

Courtly, she felt sure, was a really kind woman ; and, moreover, so appreciative, so amusing, and so many-sided, that Grace found it impossible to resist her charm. What a blessed gift (taking too low a stand among the virtues, indeed, not regarded as a virtue at all, by some) is tact ! Mrs. Courtly possessed it in a conspicuous degree. She never said anything to wound the susceptibilities of her audience: whereas Mrs. Van Winkle, clever as she was, never seemed to have any perception of when she might, with impunity, astonish her audience, and when it would be wiser to sacrifice that keen but momentary enjoyment. Vanity, and a desire to maintain her reputation for audacious wit, rendered her case-hardened against shocked looks. She said to Grace,—

"You know, the very last person with whom one should be seen in New York society is one's husband. Now, I started very badly. I began married life by being really in love with mine, and, socially, it nearly ruined me. It has taken me fifteen years to live it down, and I am only just recovering from the fatal mistake I made."

The girl knew exactly what value to attach

to such utterances as these. She never gratified the speaker by looking surprised.

Grace stood on the deck with Saul Barham as the *Teutonic* slowly, almost imperceptibly, neared the landing-wharf. A thick fog had shrouded the great statue of America, the shores of New Jersey, Staten Island, and all the features of the beautiful sea-avenue to New York.

" I am angry," said Barham, " that you should not have a better impression of the city on landing. It is too bad to have a fog here to greet you that is worthy of London."

" A delicate attention on the part of America to make us Britishers feel ' at home. ' "

" I hope you will appreciate all such attentions," he returned, smiling, " and not be too much influenced by first impressions. Ladies, I believe, generally are."

" And men ? "

" Well, a man—at all events, an American— is slower in forming any in his intercourse with foreigners. You see, English manners are different in some ways from ours ; it wouldn't do for us to trust first impressions very often."

" Has your remark any personal application ? "

asked Grace, laughing. " Did my manners repel you at first ? "

" No," he replied, quietly ; " I had never met a young lady like you, and, yet, I can't exactly say why ; for your manners have more of the frankness of our nicest American girls than those of the most Englishwomen I have met ; and English*men*—well, as I say—they require to be known."

Miss Ballinger was silent. She felt sure that her brother's free-and-easy, rather *de haut en bas* manner was in the sensitive young American's mind. She knew also what a good fellow Mordaunt really was at heart, and how either man, if he could discard his husk, would appreciate the other. But the husk of manner is as necessary a protection to the Englishman, who is habitually on the defensive, as the un-fashionable clothes worn by the American were to his body. She hoped these two would draw nearer to each other by-and-by, but at present there was nothing to be done. Pre-sently he said,—

" That Lady Clydesdale, is she really a great lady ? Her opinions and her manners seem to us rather odd."

"I wish I could say she is not well-born, but she is. I shouldn't mind her opinions if she had only better manners. Such an incendiary should at least offer her fire-brands with some persuasive charm, not fling them in your face; pray don't regard her as a typical English-woman. I am ashamed of my countrywoman."

He smiled.

"And, yet, I fancy she will have great success with some of our advanced women. When are you coming to Boston, Miss Ballinger?"

"I have no idea, but I shall let you know as soon as we arrive. I have promised Mrs. Barham to go out and spend a day at your father's house. It will interest me to see something of your New England village life."

"Well," he began, hesitatingly, "I will not discourage you. Mother will love dearly to receive you, but you must not expect anything like an English village, or—or the comforts of an English rectory. Things are much simpler with us, and quite different."

"I am prepared for that. If they were not different they would not interest me, though, indeed, all that concerns your mother would

interest me. I took to her at once—I told
you so—and, in that case, my first impressions
have strengthened more and more."

He replied gravely,—

"Our having met you, Miss Ballinger, your
having spoken to my mother has made a great
difference in our voyage. I shall never forget
it. When we meet again it will probably not
be on the same terms. How can it be, in a
great city? I shall call, and you will be kind
enough to say you are glad to see me—but the
informal intimacy of our long talks on deck;
can it be renewed on shore? I think not.
Still, I shall always look back to those hours
as quite some of the most delightful in my life."

"I hope they will be renewed. I assure
you I shall always remember them with the
greatest pleasure."

"Ah! you have many such pleasant memo-
ries, no doubt. I have very few."

The crowd, the shouts of porters, emissaries
from hotels, and friends of passengers, who
now rushed on board, put an end to further
conversation. Grace had only time to bid him
and his mother good-bye (she had already
taken leave of her other friends), when she was

hurried off by her brother to the carriage which was waiting to take them to the hotel.

And here I will seize the opportunity, while our travellers are landing, of saying a few words as to the Ballinger family, which will make the position of this brother and sister more easily understood.

Sir Henry Ballinger, who died only two years ago, was, as everyone knows, a remarkable man; prominent in politics, he had been twice a cabinet minister, distinguished as an author upon currency and international law, absorbed in the frigid, more than in the burning questions of the day; but, still, so much absorbed as to have little leisure to bestow upon his children. Their mother died when Mordaunt was sixteen and Grace was twelve; and what they would have done without Mrs. Frampton, their father's sister, who almost took Lady Ballinger's place in the household from that time forward, it is hard to say. Mordaunt was at Eton; he was an impressionable lad, who stood too much in awe of his father ever to make a friend of him, and to whom the loss of a mother's sympathy meant more than it would to many boys. He was

much less clever than his sister, but possessed
far more "worldly wisdom," as it is called,
which, from a high standpoint, is probably
nearer akin to foolishness. Nevertheless, he
had a capacity for strong attachment; and,
as a boy, his mother had been everything to
him. He was very fond of his sister, and
as years advanced, she became more and
more prominent in his life, but at this time she
was too young to be his companion, still less
his confidante. Happily Mordaunt and his aunt
had always been great friends. He used to
say he could talk more easily with her than
with anyone; her plane of wisdom was not too
far above him. Soon after Lady Ballinger's
death, Mrs. Frampton arrived on a long visit;
and from that time filled the vacant place at the
head of the table during several months each
year. She had her own house in London, and,
when resident there, the two establishments
were separate; but when Sir Henry moved to
the country, or if he took Grace abroad, Mrs.
Frampton always accompanied them. Between
the aunt and niece there was also a strong
affection; but Grace's nature being less plas-
tic than her brother's, Mrs. Frampton's influence

was less than it was upon Mordaunt. As
the girl grew up, the difference of opinion on
many points between her aunt and herself
grew more marked. It did not prevent their
being the best of friends; but their way of
looking at many questions was diametrically
opposed. Intellectually, Mrs. Frampton and
her niece had much in common; but Mordaunt
had that respect for his aunt's judgment which
led him to consult her upon points where
Grace would have decided for herself, and
decided differently.

Grace's education had been a broken one;
now sent to a foreign school for a year,
when her father went to Australia, now left in
her aunt's charge, to the tuition of governesses
and masters. It is doubtful whether she had
profited much by either. What she was she
had made herself, more than had been made by
instruction. She was not accomplished; but
her bright, quick intelligence, and keen delight
in books, stood her in good stead, in her intercourse with all the clever men who flocked to
her father's house. She had been in the world
five years when he died, and was now nearly
six-and-twenty. Early youth had had for her

its usual illusions, its usual disappointments, but they had not embittered, they had only strengthened the sweet, fresh nature, which retained a healthy capacity for enjoyment.

Within the past year she had suffered the keenest trouble she had yet known, and, consequent upon this, and upon their divergent views, had occurred the nearest approach to estrangement between aunt and niece which they had ever known. It is not necessary in this place to enter into the nature of the cloud which had arisen, and had darkened the sky in that small household, Of course Mordaunt Ballinger sided with his aunt: he always did, in any family discussion ; and Grace consequently pent up her hopes, and her disappointments, in silence, and with a brave face, that told nothing. She did not go quite so much into the world during the following months, neither would she altogether shun society ; and when the suggestion came from Mordaunt that she and Mrs. Frampton should accompany him to America, she hailed the idea. Change of scene, change of people, change of thought, she felt that all this was the best thing for her just now.

Mrs. Frampton was an odd combination of
the child of nature and the woman of the world.
Clever, impulsive, strong in her affections,
unjust and implacable in her hatreds, often
humorous, sometimes sarcastic, even at her
own expense, she possessed an extraordinarily
sound clear judgment in all business matters,
and such as concerned temporal welfare and
advancement. There was no sacrifice she would
not have made for her nephew and niece; but
her devotion to Grace was perhaps even greater
than to Mordaunt, though between him and
herself there had never been a difference, and
between her and Grace so many. This last
subject of division, and the withdrawal of Grace's
confidence, the feeling that there was one for-
bidden subject between them, had tried the
elder woman sorely. She had been very bitter
about it, until Grace's demeanour had shown
her that there could no longer be any discussion;
if she attempted to renew it, her niece left the
room. In her inward heart, she admired the
noble-minded, resolute girl all the more for her
attitude; though she never admitted that she
did so. She spoke of it to Mordaunt as " re-
prehensible folly," which was justly punished,

" but, thank goodness! there is an end, once and for ever, to all *that.*" She was delightfully inconsistent; it made her the amusing and provoking person she was; in all that did not pertain to hard-headed calculation, and worldly perspicacity.

Mordaunt Ballinger found himself, at his father's death, with all the expensive habits that are bred in the life he was leading, and but very moderate means. Sir Henry's pension of course died with him; so did a considerable income which he had enjoyed as chairman of certain railway and other companies. His son resolved to let his country-house, which was too expensive for him to keep up; and he left the Guards. The constituency which his father had represented, offered to nominate him in the late baronet's place, and after a little hesitation he accepted the proposal, and was elected. These steps he had not taken without consulting Mrs. Frampton, whose influence had also been wisely exercised in restraining him from embarking in sundry speculations. His thoughts had now been turned for some time past to America, as an Eldorado where he might improve his fortunes, as certain friends of

his had done. Not that he meant to give up
Parliament, leave England, and all it pleasures,
and live upon a ranche. That would not have
suited Mordaunt at all. But there was "real
estate" in some of the rising cities, silver mines,
shares in canned-meat companies, railways,
tramways, waterworks, surely in some of these
he might find a good investment that would
bring him in eight or ten per cent? Mrs.
Frampton's present terror was that her nephew
would be induced by some designing person to
risk considerable sums in that land of reckless
speculation. When he proposed, therefore, that
she and Grace should accompany him on a
visit to the United States, she jumped at the
suggestion. To see the Americans *chez eux*
was the thing of all others she had always
wished. It was odd that she had never been
heard to express the wish before, but no one
was surprised at anything Mrs. Frampton said.
She suddenly remembered that she had some
dear friends, the Hurlstones, in New York. It
was eight years since she had seen or heard of
them, but she would write to them at once ; she
felt sure they would do all in their power to
make New York pleasant to herself and her

belongings.   But, as to that, her brother's—Sir
Henry's—name was sure to secure them a warm
welcome in a country where he had been so
well known, and Mordaunt's being in Parliament
would be an additional reason.   It would be
charming, too, for Grace ; it would change
the current of her thoughts.   She only said this
to Mordaunt, but the alacrity with which his
sister acceded to the proposition told him and
his aunt that she felt this to be true.

Unfortunately, within a week of their sailing,
just before Christmas, Mrs. Frampton was sum-
moned, by telegram, to Geneva, by a sister of
her late husband's.   The message stated that
Miss Frampton was dying, and desired her
sister-in-law's presence.   Mrs. Frampton felt
she had no choice but to obey.   It was unfor-
tunate!   Had it only come a few days later!   As
it was, there was nothing for it but to start
by the next train, and let Mordaunt and Grace
sail for New York without her.   She promised to follow them, if Mordaunt resolved to
remain all the winter in the States.   And, on
the other hand, she extracted a promise from
him, to embark in no scheme without con-

sulting her. With this understanding they parted, hurriedly and sorrowfully, and a fortnight from the day when they had seen her into the train at Charing Cross, they landed at New York.

CHAPTER V.

THE day after her arrival, this is the letter Miss Ballinger wrote to Mrs. Frampton :—

9th January, 1891.

DEAREST AUNT SUSAN,—We were delighted to have your telegram just before starting, saying that Miss Frampton had rallied. I hope that her recovery will be so rapid as to enable you to leave her before many weeks are over. We miss you terribly, and shall do so, now that we have landed, more than ever. The voyage was really delightful, I never could have believed it would have gone so quickly, and I had such an appetite, dear aunt, you would have been ashamed of me, instead of scolding as you have done lately, because I ate so little. Mordy was very happy. He made friends with one man who was in pork and another in oil. I wonder which is nicest, to be in pork or in oil ? I always knew which he had been pounding the deck with, by his coming up to me afterwards and saying, " Do you know, I'm thinking seriously of going into pork," or " oil," as the case might be. Then he fell in love with a dear woman nearly old enough to be his mother, a Mrs. Courtly, whom most of the other women hated and abused, particularly odious Lady Clydesdale, who was on board. The things she said to me about her!—I replied that Mrs. Courtly's only crime, as far as I could see, was that she succeeded in attracting people, " And it is a pity more women don't try," I added. " They might at least *try*. For my part, my only serious aim in life is to make as many people like me as ever I can." You should have seen her face of ineffable scorn as she turned away. You always say I am so toast-and-watery, aunt, that I can't hate. I have at last accomplished it ; congratulate me ; I really do hate Lady Clydesdale. Among those on board whom I liked was an odd, clever man named Ferrars. He would puzzle, and, I believe, interest you. His past is mysterious, he never speaks of it, nor, indeed, of his present,

for that matter. I discovered, by that exhaustive process of pumping which Mordy
declares qualifies me to become a female inter-
viewer (Oh I have something to tell you about
that, presently) that he is a Southerner, who
lives chiefly in Europe, and that he writes ; but
what, and *where*, he curtly refused to say. He
is quite indifferent to fame or money, and we
generally disagreed about everything : and yet
I got to like him. In contrast to Mr. Ferrars,
who, I am sure, is not just to his country's
future, whatever he may be to her present,
there was a young Professor from Harvard, an
ardent patriot, who could not bear a word to
be said against America. I do not feel sure
that you would like this Mr. Barham as much
as Mr. Ferrars, though he is to me much more
interesting. But he is shy, and proud, and
not very forthcoming, and you like turbulent
youth. You *might* call him " a prig," which
would distress me ; but when you saw his
mother, who is a Philadelphian, and I am certain
must be a direct descendant of William Penn—
so sweet, and drab-coloured, and gentle, with
the youngest and yet saddest face you ever
looked upon, to be the mother of this handsome

young man—I say, when you looked upon her, you would better understand why he is as he is ; you would see that repression was born in him. Then there was a very rich young man from New York, who, like the young man in Scripture, ought to be told to go and sell all that he has, he would be so much happier. But being very stupid, he doesn't know that he is not happy. He fancies the fatigue of doing nothing vigorously is enjoyment. Last of all, in our set—for you must know a steamer has its " sets " as well as a city—was the authoress of " Phryne," a rather *risky* novel which has had some success. You know how fatal it is to any but a strong head to write a moderately successful book. Mrs. Van Winkle is pretty, and good-natured, but I suppose she was born foolish ; the book has done the rest. We got through the Custom House very well, though the officer seemed to think it impossible that any " gent " could require so many " pants " as Mordy brought with him. Virginie had frightened me so by saying I should have to pay duty on all my new gowns, that I was relieved when the inquisition was over. The first impression of New York in a fog was not

favourable. Then the paving of the streets !
Words cannot describe to you the condition of
all the thoroughfares. Our London streets,
Heaven knows! are bad enough in wet
weather ; and even in dry are not above
reproach compared with Paris—but these ! the
smallest town in Bulgaria would be ashamed of
such atrocities. In some there are holes so
deep that it is necessary to put a tub or a few
stones round the gaping chasm to prevent
people falling in. In some the electric wires
were lying playfully about under the horses'
feet, a storm, I am told, having brought them
all down *more than a week ago!* In Broadway
the tramways intersect each other like the
criss-crossings on some withered old palm ; but
the line of life cannot be long, I imagine, for
anyone who resides there. We found comfortable rooms awaiting us at the hotel, but heated
by a furnace such as only Shadrach and Co.
could face. I flung open all the windows to the
manager's amazement. On the table was a
splendid bouquet of crimson roses with a note
and a card. Whose do you think ? The
Hurlstones. A very pretty attention, which I
am afraid *we* should not have thought of. To

be greeted thus on arrival by strangers, for to us they are absolute strangers, is very pleasant. The note was to ask us to dine with them to-night. Presently, another card was brought me on which was written " Miss M. T. Clutch," with a request that I would receive the lady. I innocently thought this must be another kindly disposed person, to whom friends had written, unknown to us, on our behalf. Judge of my consternation when a small, smirking woman entered, who introduced herself thus,—

" I represent *The New York Scavenger*, one of our prominent Daily's, Miss Ballinger. Your name is well known, I may say it is a household word among us. I trust you feel like answering a few questions which will be of interest to our readers ? "

" You must be mistaking me for some one else," I replied. " I am not eminent in any way, and your readers cannot possibly—" she interrupted me.

" Oh ! but you are Sir Henry Ballinger's daughter, and, as such, are quite an interesting personality in America. We thought a heap of him. We claim that his book had a bigger circulation in the States than in England."

"It is a pity, then, that the States paid him nothing for it," I said. "But do you really mean that you consider the relations of a well-known man to be public property? I have not even written a book that can be pirated. I don't lecture, or preach, or act. I am a perfectly obscure individual, whom your readers cannot possibly know anything about."

"Oh! but they *do*," she insisted. "They've seen your photograph among the society beauties, they've read your name in the society papers, they know you belong to the tip-top swells. And then there was the report which went all the round of the States that a German prince had nearly blown out his brains for love of you."

This was more than I could stand. I rose quickly: "You must pardon me if I decline to continue this conversation. I am not accountable for all the rubbish you may have heard, but at least I will not be a party to disseminating more. Good morning."

"You might just tell me why you are come here, and—and a few other things?"

"Nothing at all. I wish to remain un-noticed."

"Well! That is real disobliging. But if you conclude to say nothing, I guess it's no good my staying."

"No," I repeated after her, "I guess it's no good."

And so she left the room. Mordy says I ought to have submitted to the infliction, and that I showed my usual want of worldly wisdom, in snubbing a reporter. But why? It is all very well for him to see these people, he has had a tribe of them after him, and it may be proper and even useful that he should see them all. But, in my case, it would be worse than ridiculous, and I think it a gross piece of im-pertinence on Miss Clutch's part, trying to force publicity upon me.

10th January.—I did not close my letter yes-terday, finding it would catch to-day's mail if I posted it this morning: and I knew you would like to hear about our dinner. The Hurlstones live in Fifth Avenue. It is a fine house, and everything about it is very grand—more grand, perhaps, than comfortable, according to our ideas. Americans have always been ruled by

French taste, not only in dress, but in art, and in certain social matters. The old French idea of a *salon* prevails here: gorgeous furniture; but no books, no writing-table, no evidences of occupation, except a grand piano, shrouded in some rare gold-woven tapestry. A few pictures by Corot, Daubigny, and Troyon adorn the walls. A bust of Mrs. Hurlstone by D'Epinay, with a bunch of roses in her hair, a necklace and a lace *fichu* over her shoulders stands in the window. The two ladies were dressed, like their home, in the perfection of French taste. You know the father and mother, who is still handsome, so I need not describe them; but the daughter has grown up since they were in England, and is considered a beauty. She has delicate features, fine eyes, and pretty, though not brilliant colouring. She is intelligent, vivacious, and meets one more than half way in her desire to be agreeable, as few English girls of eighteen would be able to do. She has, moreover, no twang; no ugly intonations of voice. Why don't I admire her more? I kept asking myself this, as I watched her. Though set off by dress to the best advantage, for some reason she does not produce the effect she should. There is one son, a year older, equally good-looking, perhaps even handsomer; but of that order of beauty that leaves no impression. I have already forgotten what he was like, except that he wore a very large diamond in his shirt-front. The father took me in to dinner. I like him exceedingly, perhaps the best of the family; but all were most amiable. We were sixteen at dinner. Nearly every other guest was actually, or prospectively, a millionaire. The women were all very well dressed, and wore a great many jewels, more than perhaps we should think quite good taste for this sort of party. They were one and all extremely civil; offering to take me out driving, and so on. One of them, a Mrs. Siebel, married to a wealthy banker of German origin, was particularly bright and amusing. I felt as if I knew her better in half an hour than I have ever done an Englishwoman in the same time. Another, Mrs. Thorley, who is the sovereign of all social entertainments here, was most gracious. She is going to give a great ball to which she invited us. Some of the men struck me as clever, especially in conversation with

their own countrywomen, their quickness and
incisiveness were remarkable. With me they
seemed a little stiff, a little on their p's and q's.
One of the exceptions was a man whom they
called 'George Ray, the Third.' When I inquired the reason of this curious appellation, I
was told it was because his father and grand-
father, both alive, were also Georges. He is a
splendid animal; and he knows it. *He* certainly cannot be accused of being stiff. He
planted his chair opposite me, leant his elbows
on his knees, and told me of all the great people
he knew in London, as though he thought that
was the only topic that would interest me.
This was not clever on George the Third's part.
And yet he was anything but dull; and his
perfect self-satisfaction entertained me. Mrs.
Hurlstone seemed afraid he might prove peril-
ously entertaining. She was good enough to
inform me that he had not a penny, he had run
through everything. It was considerate of her.
A much more amusing man, however, sat next
me at dinner; a barrister, named Sims, shrewd
and humorous. I asked him who a little red-
haired man with a waxed moustache, opposite,
was; evidently a foreigner. He replied, ' He

is Jean Jacques, Marquis de Tréfeuille, a *pair de France* of the first water, who is come over here to hitch on to an heiress, if he can. It was of him that some wag wrote,—

"Tu es Jean, tu es Jacques, tu es roux, tu es sot,
Mais tu n'es pas Jean Jacques Rousseaux!"

I inquired if the girl next him was the future Marquise. He shook his head : " I doubt it. Even if she tumbles to the coronet, he will find her father won't make the settlement the Marquis expects. He will give her a big allowance, but not a lump sum down, and I doubt if that will suit the Marquis." Before the evening was over, Mr. Sims asked Mordy and me to dine with him at Delmonico's, next week. I have time for no more.

Your ever affectionate niece,

GRACE BALLINGER.

P.S.—Mordy says he will write to you by the next mail. He is already up to his eyes in engagements, and made a great deal of, a great deal *more* of than he is in London, so no wonder he likes it.

Second P.S.—Mordy has just run in, shouting with laughter, this morning's *Scavenger* in his hand. "Here you are!" he cried, "and serve you right!" Then he read the cutting (I am not sunk so low as to mean a pun) which I enclose. I hope it will amuse you, as much as it did *him*.

The paragraph was as follows :—

" Sir Mordaunt Ballinger, Baronet and M.P., with his sister landed here from the *Teutonic* yesterday. She is credited with being a London belle, and, as such, and the daughter of one of the few Englishmen who have not written gross falsehoods concerning our country, we were desirous of interviewing her ; but the young woman, with a rudeness peculiarly British, re-fused to submit to any interrogation. If she is a specimen of London's beauty, we cannot congratulate that city on its show. A Grenadier in petticoats, quite wanting in the delicacy and elegance we consider essential for beauty, best describes her. She is decidedly too fleshy. Her hair is not stylishly coifed, and there is a slip-sloppiness about her attire which denotes that she is not gowned in Paris. Altogether, we have seldom experienced a greater dis-appointment both as to appearance and manner, in a woman of whom we had been taught to expect so much."

CHAPTER VI.

SIR MORDAUNT BALLINGER was indeed, as his sister had said, made a great deal of in New York society. It took but a few days to accomplish this. From the square business-like letters, to the blush-coloured note, documents poured in on him all day long. There were invitations from men to lunch at the " Lawyers' Club down town," to meet railway directors, promoters of mines, and others " who can give you information concerning," etc., etc. There were formal cards requesting his presence at great club dinners and private banquets ; and there were informal beckons to every species of entertainment, from four o'clock teas upwards. No stranger in London ever found himself so swiftly and surely swept away on a tide of hospitality. Mrs. Frampton had rightly predicted that her brother's name would be an

"open sesame" to his son and daughter ; for
Grace was not left out of all this cordial
welcome. Ladies' luncheons, "to meet Miss
Ballinger," theatre parties, receptions, diver-
sions of all kinds were offered her. Still, it was
not to be expected that she should be made
quite so much fuss with as her brother. He
was in some sense a public man. His name
and position as his father's successor and an
M.P. carried a certain weight, and then he was
good-looking, with invariably charming manners to women, and variably attractive ones to
men, with a genuine relish of a joke, which
made him popular after dinner among those
who told good stories, and where is the sharp
American who has not a store of them ? For
serious, practical purposes, however, these gifts
did not, as a certain May Clayton told him,
"amount to much.".

"You're a lovely man to flirt with, but unless
you find a girl with a pile, you're not eligible as
a husband, you see."

May Clayton was a young lady whom he
met at that dinner Mr. Sims gave at
Delmonico's. She was a "bud," as Mr. Sims
informed his English friends ; that is, she was

only just formally introduced to society. But, owing to her education, she had no shyness or diffidence, and in knowledge of the world and effrontery of speech might have been a woman of forty. She could not remember the time when she had not had flirtations, had not been escorted back from daily school by youthful beaux, had not been to parties every week, and received bouquets and bonbons. It was astonishing she should be as captivating as she was, with all the bloom of youth rubbed off her, and her speech interlarded with slang. But she was pretty, quick-witted, and her exuberant spirits were especially attractive to English people, who have so little gas in themselves, they are glad to be lit, and their stock replenished by others. She and a Mrs. Flynn were the only ladies besides Grace. Both of them could tell who their grandfathers were; both had connections who were among the "400," and yet neither was in what Mr. Sims called "the swim." They went to the Assembly and Patriarch balls, but the great leaders of society knew them not; they had not learned as yet to ingratiate themselves with the venerable leader of cotillons, Mrs.

Flynn not being rich enough to give balls herself. They were cousins. Mr. Flynn had
something to do with steel plates, and had
failed twice. Perhaps this was why his pretty
little wife had also failed. He rarely went into
society, nor did Mrs. Clayton when she could
avoid it, being apparently shelved as completely as though she were defunct. Her
daughter already received visits, gave parties,
and went everywhere either with Mrs. Flynn or
alone to houses where there was a matron.
She told Sir Mordaunt she expected him to
call, " And mind, you're not to ask for mamma,
but for me." And to Grace she said, " You're
just as nice as ever you can be, and I hope
you'll come and see me, but not with your
brother." May was bright, and cheery, and
shrill as a canary. She chirped and trilled
away, drowning everyone else's voice, even
those of the young American men of the party,
though they were jovial, high-spirited fellows,
fully able to hold their own. She told one of
them who was boasting a little, to " come off
that roof ! " To Ballinger, who said something
about the breast and the leg of a chicken, she
said, " *We* always call it ' the brown meat,
and white meat."

"Would not that sound rather odd, if applied to the human form?" he asked, with apparent innocence.

"Well! To be sure—I never thought of that!"

Then she seemed about to illustrate this by an example, but only laughed and turned the subject.

Being challenged, she sang a stave of some "Darkey" song, to the delight of her auditors, then suddenly stopped, "No, it isn't nice. I won't sing any more," nor could any supplications induce her to continue. The audacious, wayward little creature had evidently clearly defined limits of her own, beyond which her high spirits never transgressed, no matter what encouragement she met. And her admirers understood this. They drew her out, and roared at her sallies, but there was no suspicion of license in the familiarity which was nevertheless unlike anything to which the English guests had been accustomed.

"Have they all been brought up together?" Miss Ballinger asked her host.

"Oh, no. She is a Kentucky girl, only came here this winter. They probably danced

the German together for the first time a few
weeks ago. I asked her and Mrs. Flynn,
because I thought it would amuse you more to
meet two individual types of Americans—of a
certain stamp—as they are before the edge is
taken off them, than the smart conventional
women, such as we met the other night, who
are much the same all the world over. You
don't object ? "

" On the contrary ; I much prefer it. I am
all for different nations having a different code
of manners. I don't see why we are all to be
built up on the same pattern."

Mr. Sims laughed.

" Don't run away with the impression that
this is the general code of manners. No ; they
belong to a certain type, a type which you
English enjoy more than some of our own
countrymen do, especially the Anglomaniacs.
We shall soon have all the originality rubbed
out of us. There is Mrs. Flynn. She was
twice as amusing a year or two ago. Now she
is afraid to let herself *go*. She is eating her
heart out, poor little woman, because she
doesn't get on. I'm afraid she is going in for
the ' prunes and prism ' business.

"I shouldn't have thought it," said Miss Ballinger smiling, as she glanced at the graceful little woman, who was carrying on a lively flirtation with Mordaunt.

After dinner they went to the theatre, where their host had taken a row of stalls, in order that his guests might see a thoroughly representative American play. Viewed as a literary production, the piece was amazing. But the capital picture of American country life, the naturalness of the characters, the humour and pathos of the acting in these scenes, redeemed that portion which was supposed to depict the graces and the vices of the moneyed aristocracy of New York. It seemed curious to Grace that the actors and actresses should not have caught even the faintest outward resemblance to ladies and gentlemen. On this point, however, her American acquaintances were more indignant, more bitter in ridicule than herself.

Mordaunt Ballinger told his sister, as they drove home, that New York was an awfully nice place. He believed he was being put up to a good thing or two, and he should be in no hurry to go away. Grace assured him she was quite content to remain there as long as he

liked. " Only don't fall in love with Miss
Clayton," she added, laughing. " I don't think
Aunt Susan *could* stand her for a niece."

He laughed in return. " She is very fetching.
Why is it that no English girl has that *abandon* ?
But you needn't be afraid ; she is too cute to
marry a pauper. She warned me that I wasn't
eligible. Fancy an English girl doing that !
As Sims said (Sims is a deuced clever fellow),
' American women are like pins. Their heads
will always prevent them from being lost, plunge
they never so deep ! ' "

Quintin Ferrars called on the Ballingers the day
after their arrival. He was remaining on in New
York ; for what purpose did not seem very clear,
as he had told Grace, during the voyage, that
business in Virginia was bringing him over, and
that nothing but business would have induced
him to come at this season. Nor had he any
friends in New York. He seemed as much
a stranger there as the Ballingers ; indeed,
more so ; for they had invitations, and he had
none, and spoke with profound aversion of New
York Society. He visited with them the
Metropolitan Museum of Art, some exhibitions
of modern pictures, and several private collec-

tions, which they had obtained permission to
see. They also accompanied him to Daly's
Theatre, where some of those slight comedies
in which the canvas was nothing and the work
thereon perfection were being performed. His
remarks were always trenchant and original ;
his satire sometimes pungent. But it seemed
to Grace that the man was more depressed and
at times more bitter than he had appeared during
the passage. The one thing which she did not
see was that he was in love with her. Mordaunt,
with not half her perspicacity, saw it, but held
his peace. Grace had too recently had a
bitter disappointment, for him to fear that she
would fall in love with the first middle-aged
American who laid his heart and fortune at her
feet. Still, it was well that he should make
inquiries touching this Ferrars. But he could
learn little or nothing. Those he asked said the
man came of a good old Virginian stock, and
was well off. But he had not lived in America
for many years ; during his occasional visits,
few saw him ; if anything was to be known of
his life, it was not in New York.

About Gunning, on the other hand, who had
been unremitting in his attentions to Grace

ever since their arrival, there were no inquiries to be made. He had proposed Sir
Mordaunt as a visitor to the Knickerbocker and
Manhattan Athletic Clubs. There and else-
where everyone spoke well of the young man.
He did not drink ; he did not gamble ; he had
never been known to do a shabby thing. He
was manly, straightforward, and liberal with his
money. To his mother, who lived with him,
he was an excellent son ; to his companions a
generous friend. He was not always "very
good form ; " but Ballinger had seen worse
failings than a little bombast, a little empty
talk, knocked out of a man. He certainly did
not wish his sister to marry an American, he
said to himself ; but if she should have a fancy
that way, it would be as well if she would select
one for whom everyone had a good word, and
who possessed a million of dollars a year.

Here is a passage from a letter to his aunt.

"People say no American man ever *really*
likes an Englishman. Some of the young
fellows may be a little jealous of a stranger, if
he has any success here ; but all I know is that
most of them have been awfully kind to me ;
and many of them are capital company. I

daresay one mustn't inquire too curiously how
some of these great fortunes were made; that
is no concern of mine. They all seem very
glad to put one in the way of making a good
thing. One fellow tells me that orange groves
or fruit orchards in Southern California are the
safest investments; giving the largest returns,
from 25 to 40 per cent., on the capital laid out.
Another advises "reel estate," as they call it,
near one of the rising cities (mining centres) in
Colorado. He says land can't fail to double or
treble in value; only one must be content to let
the money remain tied up for a time. A third
recommends a Mexican opal mine which he says
he knows is a first-rate thing. But the man
I am most disposed to trust is a shrewd chap
named Reid, to whom I brought a letter. He
has been awfully kind, explaining things. He
says there is nothing like being on the spot;
and recommends strongly my going out West,
and looking into these various investments.
He has been explaining to me how the whole
city is ruled by the Irish vote, and what awful
corruption goes on. Talk of liberty! It seems
to me they have precious little here; everything
is sacrificed to party. And the worst of it is,

the best men stand aloof. Fellows of high
character and enormous wealth, who ought to
have the chief weight in municipal matters, have
none. They won't mix themselves up with the
Irish, whom they hate. Apropos of Americans,
the greatest *parti* in New York, a young chap
named Gunning, is awfully gone on Grace. He
crossed with us, and it began then; but she
would have nothing to say to him, preferring
the society of a man nearly old enough to be
her father, named Ferrars (so like her, isn't it?)
or of a thin, pasty-looking young professor, in
horribly made overalls, and a reach-me-down.
Gracey always *will* be queer in her tastes, to the
end of the chapter! Flowers come every
morning from this Gunning. She can't return
them; but she declines every other mortal thing
he offers, his riding horses, carriages, theatre-
parties, &c. I have had difficulty in getting
her to accept a party he is giving "to meet
Miss Ballinger,"—that is the New York form,
when they want to do a person special honour.
He heard her say she would like to see a
Spanish dancer who is here, and who only per-
forms at a low *café*, where ladies can't go; but
occasionally dances at private houses for a

select circle. That is how he caught her. I wish I could see that she took any interest in any-one *particularly*—that there was any symptom of her *having forgotten*. She is always cheery, always ready for everything ;—but, by-the-bye, have you heard when the trial is to take place ? I hope soon, while we are over here. It would be much better that Grace should not be in England when it comes off. It would worry her, and rake up the past. Well ! I hope you are coming out to us soon. We both want you awfully."

On the subject of invitations I may here give a characteristic note which Miss Ballinger received a few days after their arrival :—

MY DEAR MISS BALLINGER,—Will you and your brother give me the pleasure of your company at a blue dinner on the 28th of January, at 8 o'clock ? I have selected this colour, not because I am called a " blue-stocking " by those who are amazed that a woman should know Greek, but to honour you and the country I adore. I shall never rest till Mr. Van Winkle is appointed Minister to Saint James's. I believe your Queen would be gratified by having at her court one woman representative alike of literature and fashion.

Your true-blue friend,

CORRINA VAN WINKLE.

This dinner had not yet come off. In the meantime Mordaunt and Grace went in the Hurlstones' box one night to hear "Siegfried." The box was a large one, on the grand tier, and besides the Hurlstone ladies, and the Ballingers, there were Gunning, and another of the *jeunesse dorée* of New York. Grace had heard that society was enthusiastic about Wagner's music, and that there was a great difficulty in obtaining a good opera-box, for which far larger sums were paid than are ever given in England. She innocently imagined that people went to listen to the music ; she was undeceived. She had petitioned to go early, as she had never heard "Siegfried," and she and Mordaunt were in the box nearly an hour before the owners of it arrived. At first all was well. The upper boxes were crowded by Germans, who listened devoutly to every note ; so did the unfashionable occupants of the stalls in their morning dress. But in the middle of the second act the grand tier,

which till then had been nearly empty, filled
rapidly with smart ladies and their attendant
cavaliers, and from that time onward a continu-
ous fire of conversation was kept up, without
even the semblance of any attention to the
orchestra or the stage. That was the only part
of the theatre to which opera-glasses seemed
rarely to be directed. They raked every box,
and the Hurlstones', by reason of its stranger
guests, more persistently than any other. In
vain Grace fixed her eyes alternately on
the book of the words and on the stage. In
vain there were angry expostulations from the
stalls of " Stop that talking!" Miss Hurlstone
actually turned round deliberately and sat with
her back to the house, talking to the Marquis
de Tréfeuille and a number of other young
men who flocked in and out; and in doing
this she was only following the example of
others. To listen to the lightest French
or Italian opera under such conditions would
have been impossible; but when the music
was Wagner's, music which demands the
strain of every nerve, the tension of every intellectual faculty to grasp the meaning of that
tumult of sound, to follow and seize the floating

gossamers of melody from the brambles of apparent discord, it was nothing short of exasperating. It became sound and fury, signifying nothing. Grace recalled the darkness, the death-like silence of the theatre at Bayreuth. If Wagner could have risen from the grave to see himself so treated! She gave it up at last in despair, as Mrs. Hurlstone leant forward for the fourth time (Gunning had been pouring his thin stream of small talk over her shoulder), and said,—

"There is the Princess Lamperti just come in with George Ray—that fat woman in black, with yellow pompons and pearls. You know her history, poor thing! She was Miss Morse of Baltimore, and fell in love with the prince at Rome. He married her for her money, and he behaved very ill. They were married more than ten years; there was never a word said against her, but, after a miserable life, she has at last divorced him on the ground of his desertion, at his solicitation, they say, in order that he may marry some Spanish woman to whom he has long been devoted, and who is also very rich. Dreadful, isn't it? Everyone feels very much for the poor princess."

Here Gunning, who had heard part of Mrs. Hurlstone's narration, said,—

"You know the prince, I suppose, Mrs. Hurlstone? Look up at the third box on the second tier. You'll see him there behind a very dark lady—I suppose Madame Moretto."

"You don't mean that he has had the effrontery to come here, when he knew his wife was in New York?"

"Why not? They're divorced; and Lamperti has cheek enough for anything. I don't think they are staying in New York city, however."

Mrs. Hurlstone, whose glass had been riveted on the box during this speech, exclaimed,—

"It is the prince, sure enough! Well, I never heard anything like it, flying in the face of public opinion like that! Of course, every one will cut him. And what a coarse-looking creature Madame Moretto is! What on earth brings them *here* ?"

"I am sure I don't know. Perhaps it has something to do with the settlement of the princess's money."

"Why, it must all have been settled when

she married. You don't suppose she would give him anything more ? He has got enough out of her already. Besides, I thought this Madame Moretto was also very rich ? "

" So I conclude. He wouldn't have married her without."

" He is, then, actually married to her ? "

" Why, certainly—or, if not married, going to be."

"Upon my honour! It is a pretty story altogether. We pride ourselves upon our society being very free from scandals; but if people *will* marry foreigners," then she corrected herself, " I mean foreign princes, who are mere fortune-hunters, what can one expect ? "

Grace, meantime, had looked at the rivals in this pitiful story, and had come to the conclusion that Madame Moretto's was no common face. She was handsome, though young no longer, but the strength of the countenance, more than its beauty, made it remarkable. A woman, this, to exercise a fateful hold, probably, over any man on whom she had fastened; certainly over a weak one. As Grace looked at those eyes, burning like lamps, in the depths of two dark caverns, at the proud and splen-

didly poised head and ample bust, and then at
the figure and face of the deserted wife, she
read at once how unequal the contest must
have been. Coarse ? Well, she might be
coarse, but it was the coarse strength of
Tintoret, as compared with the faded feebleness
of Guido.

The curtain had now fallen upon the second
act, and Mordaunt, with the other men, had left
the box to visit their acquaintances and make
room for those who wished to pay their respects
to Mrs. Hurlstone and inspect the English
beauty more closely. Among these was a
powerfully built young man, of medium height,
with a fine resolute face and a delightfully
frank smile. His general bearing and ease of
manner, which never touched the confines of
familiarity, that snare of the underbred, would
have distinguished him in any society. He was
greeted with cordiality by mother and daughter,
and introduced to Miss Ballinger as Mr. Caldwell. He repeated her name, as all Americans
do, on being presented.

" Mr. Caldwell does not ,honour New York
very much," explained Mrs. Hurlstone, with a
smile. " We spoil him so much here, when-

ever he comes, that he thinks it best to make himself precious."

"Quite true," said the young fellow, showing the whitest teeth in the world, under his incipient black moustache. "It is only coming here very seldom that makes me tolerated, I know. I am a grub, an earth-worm who is out of place among the butterflies."

"What nonsense!" exclaimed Miss Hurlstone. "You know quite well that you despise us butterflies. You prefer being a grub in those horrid mines all the time, and won't come out of your chrysalis. It's too bad!"

"That is all very well, Miss Hurlstone, but how would the butterflies ever exist but for the state of grubdom? Perhaps I shall burst my chrysalis some day and flutter up and be a giddy old butterfly, but I am afraid you will have nothing to say to me then."

"Nothing!" said the young lady decisively; "if you will not when you may," and the battledore and shuttlecock of chaff went on, while Mrs. Hurlstone, who had been sweeping the house with her opera-glass, said to Grace,—

"Who are the people whose box Sir Mordaunt is in?"

Grace felt sure Mrs. Hurlstone knew.

"Mrs. Flynn and Miss Clayton. Have you never met them?"

"Oh, I believe I have met them, but they are not in our set. I fancy they are from Kentucky."

"There is no objection to that, is there?" asked Grace, with apparent innocence. "If Kentucky can produce such pretty women, I congratulate Kentucky."

"Pretty, yes; but such style! You English, my dear Miss Ballinger, are so very odd. You take up people that *we* should never know! You do that all the time in England. We hear of such extraordinary people being received there. It does seem so strange to *us*."

Grace recognized some truth in what Mrs. Hurlstone said. Probably, if she were American, she would feel much as Mrs. Hurlstone did. But she felt sure these young women were quite harmless; they had amused her; in a certain way, she had liked them; she was too loyal to give them up. So when Mrs. Hurlstone followed up her remark with,—

"Do tell me where you made Mrs. Flynn's acquaintance?"

Grace replied,—

"At a dinner your friend, Mr. Sims, gave us at Delmonico's. Is there any reason why he should not have asked them?"

"Oh, no reason exactly, except that, as a man of the world, he ought to have known they were not the kind of people you ought to meet as good specimens of New York society. I am sorry you should meet any but our best people."

Grace checked the question, "What are the best? The richest?" which rose to her lips, and said,—

"Mr. Sims thought we should be more entertained by meeting some American types such as we have not seen in England, and he was right. Miss Clayton especially amused us both very much."

"We don't like our English friends to be *amused* in that way," said Mrs. Hurlstone, with trenchant emphasis.

"Dear Mrs. Hurlstone, if everyone were alike, the world would be very dull. A little originality is so delightful. I want to see as

many different types as I can, in going through
the States. I don't think the worse of people
for not having the manners I have been used
to. Their manners are good for *them*, as mine
are for me."

" Forgive me for saying that is all nonsense,
Miss Ballinger. There is but one code of good
manners, all the world over. You will go back
to England, and quote these people, and say
that is the way Americans behave. You know
you will ! "

" Some Americans, not all," replied Grace
calmly. "And why not ? What is the use of
blinking the truth ? There are differences, you
can't deny it, and I want to see them all. The
New-Englanders, about whom I have read so
much, the warm Southerners, the wild Western-
ers, I know I shall find them all interesting in
their different ways. I don't want only to see
the smart, conventional people. I have plenty
of them at home."

Here someone entered the box, and Caldwell
rose. Then, approaching Grace, he said,—

" I believe my mother has taken the liberty
of writing to you to-night, Miss Ballinger. She
knew your father quite well, when he was over

here, and would like to make your acquaintance, but did not like to call, without writing to explain why. We shall only be quite a short time in New York; but my mother hopes she may see you."

" Certainly. I shall be charmed. If she will appoint any hour, I will be at home, or call on her."

" I will tell her. She thought, perhaps,—but no. She has written, and I will not forestall her note. I shall have the pleasure of meeting you to-morrow night at Mr. Gunning's party. Good night!"

He bowed. She extended her hand. " Do not forget my message." Then, when he had left the box, she said to her hostess, "What a charming face that young man has! So frank, and manly, and straightforward. Who is he?"

" His mother's only son. The father died two years ago, and left great mining operations in a state that required very active and constant supervision. This boy, as he was then, under-took it all, worked like a slave, and showed great cleverness, great tact and judgment, I am told, in dealing with the men, who all adore

him, I hear. He lives there in Colorado
almost entirely with his mother and a young
sister, and resists all temptations to come to
New York, unless business brings him. It is
most extraordinary."

"It is admirable. And his mother, is she as
nice as he ?"

"I don't know her. She never goes into
society here. She devotes herself to the education of her daughter, I believe, and to
making a comfortable home for her son."

But the third act had now begun, and with
it Mr. Gunning's fluid vacuity, which played
with a mild spray down Miss Ballinger's back
for the remainder of the evening.

CHAPTER VII.

THIS was what the post brought Grace the next morning :—

MY DEAR MISS BALLINGER,[1]—I hope to call on you to-morrow ; but I wish first to explain who I am. My husband was well acquainted with Sir Henry Ballinger, and he was our guest while in the United States. I am now a widow, living almost entirely in Colorado, with my son, though I have a house here. I do not go into New York society, and fear I can be of little use to you during my short stay, but if you and your brother have a spare evening, and would dine quietly with me, I would try and get one or two pleasant friends to meet you. Later on, if you are going West, it would give

---

[1] By Americans it is considered more formal, by us more familiar, to begin with "My." I am surprised to find my friend, Mr. Marian Crawford, asserting precisely the reverse in his "American Politician." I can only refer this divergence of opinion to the experience of the general reader.

me real pleasure to offer you and Sir Mordaunt
such hospitality as we can, in our wild home in
the Rocky Mountains. Should you not be at
home to-morrow, perhaps you will kindly write
and say if I am fortunate enough to find
you both disengaged any evening. All are the
same to me.

Yours sincerely,
Joanna Caldwell.

"Jem" Gunning's party that night was a
great success. He had done a good-natured
thing, by inviting Ferrars, whom he scarcely
knew, but had interchanged a few words with
on board ship, and had subsequently met at
the Ballingers. Ferrars was their friend ; he
had greatly admired Carmencita's public performances, and he had expressed a desire to
see her in private ; hence the invitation. Of
course all the very "smartest" of New York
society were there, including the Hurlstones
and Mrs. Van Winkle, and besides these, two
or three artists justly supposed to be more in
touch with the wayward, capricious dancer, who
it was said, required the enthusiasm of Bohemia
to stimulate her efforts. Before a cold, fashion-

able circle she had been known to be a failure. They had arranged the beautiful picture-gallery added by the late Mr. Gunning to his fine mansion, so that the dancer should have a little stage to herself at one end, backed by tall folding screens of Cordova leather. The electric light fell full upon this, while it was subdued in the rest of the gallery. The whole effect of the beautifully-dressed women, mostly young, not overcrowded, but seated in groups with their cavaliers, against the rich background of pictures, was in itself a little *tableau*.

Before Carmencita arrived, the Hungarian band played, and people wandered about, some to look at the pictures (which were all modern French) some to the refreshment room adjoining. Then, when it was announced that the dancer and her accompanying band of guitars had arrived, the guests were arranged in semi-circles of chairs, and, there being plenty of room for all, the men were not relegated to doorways, or flattened upright against the wall, as is generally the case in London. The band of guitars seated themselves, and began thrumming a bolero with wonderful spirit, and a body of sound that was surprising from such poor instruments. In the midst of this a young woman entered from a side door. She was dressed in white and gold, and wore a white lace mantilla over her head. She was neither pretty nor ugly, a common type of Spaniard, and her movement as she walked was swaggering. She was greeted by a great clapping of hands, which the artists led. She acknowledged this by an awkward and, as it seemed to Grace, a surly salute. Then she sat down with her feet apart, a fan in one hand, the other lying in her lap, the palm upwards. Her eyes looked dead, her whole face dull and expressionless. Could this be Carmencita? Why, the woman was not even graceful! And the smart ladies who saw her for the first time whispered, "So badly dressed! Hair so blousy, and frock gathered so fully over the hips that it makes them look ever so much too large!"

Ferrars had a chair immediately behind Grace.

"Is it possible that this is the dancer all the artist world rave about?" she asked.

"Wait."

"I can't fancy that any agility can compen-

sate for the lack of grace and charm," she
insisted.

"Wait," he again repeated. "If you are
not a convert before ten minutes are over,
write me down an ass."

The guitars had ceased their little prelude.
They were chattering to each other. The
leader's head was turned away. He had not
once glanced at Carmencita since she entered.
Now, however, he revolved upon his stool,
struck a chord, looking down as he screwed up
one string, then raised his eyes. They met
hers. It was like the falling of a spark upon
some explosive substance. Her whole face
was illuminated. She flung away her mantilla,
and rose transformed, as the guitars struck up
once more. The genius of her art had now
hold of her, and went impatiently quivering
through her frame. Her feet tapped the ground,
her arms and hands—those apathetic hands—
were lifted with a sort of exultant passion,
she drew herself proudly up, and her bolero
began.

Considered merely as dancing, probably
many of the spectators had witnessed more
wonderful performances. It was the dramatic

force, the vivid intensity of every movement that distinguished it from any ordinary terpsichorean feat. Without being what is understood as pantomimic, the little dance told its story as no dance of the kind has ever done before. When she sprang forward with that defiant audacity, bent, swayed, flung her body back till it seemed as though her head would touch the floor, her eyes appeared to flash fire, her hands and wrists in their delicate and flexible intonations played through the whole gamut of passionate emotion; they spoke with an eloquence that was not to be resisted. It was no longer a woman dancing, it was a creature possessed by some demoniac influence, struggling, supplicating, conquered; swept like a leaf before the wind, in a series of gyrations so rapid and astounding that when she sank to the earth, the spectators gasped with almost a sense of relief, amid the storm of applause that arose.

She smiled for the first time, then the light faded from her eyes, and she swaggered back to her seat, the same awkward, lumpish-looking peasant she had been ere the flame had been ignited.

"Well? What do you say?" asked Ferrars, from behind Grace's shoulder.

"Nothing. She has taken away my breath."

The flood gates were burst. "Tremendous!" "Astonishing!" "Immense!" "Did you ever see anything like that bend of body?" "There is no one can touch her!" and so on, poured the tide of frothy admiration round the room.

"They see nothing but an exhibition of agility," said Ferrars. "You see something more than this, I am sure?"

"Yes." She waited a minute, then added, "It is a physical illustration of Owen Meredith's line, 'Genius does what it must. Talent does what it can.' She could no more help dancing as she does, than a tornado can help blowing. I am not quite sure that I *like* a tornado. I think I prefer a gentler breeze. But one is carried away by the tempest, while it lasts."

"And what do you want more? To be 'carried away,' even for a few minutes, and by a dancing girl, is rare in life. I tell you that this creature has an individuality that is all her own. I have seen much more wonderful dancing in Spain, but never any that had this curious histrionic character."

" You have been in Spain much ? "

" Yes, at one time. I hope Carmencita will sing some national airs presently. She never does so in public. I hear her singing and dancing together are extraordinary. Get our host to ask her."

There was a movement at the door at this moment, and a fat, fair woman, with a sweet smile, laden with jewels, entered. Gunning went forward with his mother, and then the magnificent George Ray strode down the room, and greeted the new guest with effusion.

" Who is that ? They are going to bring her up to you," said Ferrars.

" It is the Princess Lamperti. I daresay you have heard her story. She has just divorced her husband."

They approached; and the soft cushiony-looking woman, with so complacent an expression that it was impossible to believe that her domestic sorrow had eaten deeply into her soul, was presented to Miss Ballinger. As the honoured guest of the evening, whom everyone was asked to meet, all presentations were made to her.

The princess began at once,—

" I saw you last night at the opera, Miss
Ballinger, and I was glad to think I was to
meet you to-night. Your face was very *sym-
pathcque* to me ; I am very susceptible to fresh
impressions, too much so. And you ? " But
she ran on without waiting for an answer.
" How do you like Carmencita ? Wonderful,
isn't she ? But, for me, I like something more
—more *ondoyante*—more—more—how shall I
say, ethereal ? '

The princess, though pure American, had
quite foreign terms of speech, and was much
addicted to foreign words.

" Certainly she is not ethereal," smiled
Grace. " And yet she seems a sort of
double-natured creature—a stupid peasant,
and—"

" A Paphian Priestess ! " murmured Mrs.
Van Winkle, who stood near with her head
dressed like a cockatoo. " It is like the
frenzied orgy that used to wind up some of
their interesting rites ! That intoxicating twirl
of hers at the end it is realism *in extremis*."

This sounded to Grace very like nonsense ;
but she was quick enough to respond,—

" The *extremis*, I suppose, are her head and her toes ? They were so mixed, I could not quite tell for a moment which was which."

" You know," said the princess, " that the leader of the guitars is her husband ? She adores him."

" Indeed ? That is interesting. I saw that he lit her by a look, as some people, they say, light gas by the electricity in their fingers."

" I am one of the light-fingered gentry," laughed George Ray, fatuously. " In cold weather I can always do it. I am so strongly charged with electricity."

" You are such a large battery, such a mighty machine that we are ablaze when you come near us," said Mrs. Van Winkle, with a satirical smile. Then she added reflectively, as she opened and shut her fan,—

" Fancy being lit by your own husband ! How curious ! Though once, long ago, perhaps—" Then she broke off.

" Ah ! They are so young all is new ! " sighed the princess. " One asks oneself, ' Will it continue ? ' Foreign natures are so *volages*. They know not what fidelity means, and, more than all, Italians and Spaniards ; ah ! They are a dreadful people, as I have good reason to know ! "

Grace, generally ready with her tongue, felt rather at a loss what to say.

Mrs. Van Winkle saved her.

" It must be very unexciting, dancing to your own husband. Herodias's daughter would not have won the Baptist's head under *those* circumstances. I feel like Marguerite de Valois, when she was thirsty and drank a cup of cold water, and exclaimed, ' Ah ! if it were only a sin ! ' The legitimate thing is always so very *fade*."

It was astonishing the pains this lady took to try and give a false impression of herself. But it was all thrown away on Grace.

" My aunt would have gratified Marguerite de Valois," she said. "She would have told her a cup of cold water *was* a sin—a deadly sin against hygienic laws. It is an *idée fixe* with her."

Then Mrs. Van Winkle moved on, bowing her cockatoo-like crest to right and left; and, as the princess had taken her seat, Grace turned to make some remark to Ferrars, but she saw to her surprise that he had left his chair, nor could she detect his head anywhere.

Carmencita now danced an *affondangodo*, followed by a *sequidillo*, with increasing energy, terminating by explosions, similar to that which had roused such enthusiasm in her first dance.

Young Caldwell took the vacant chair behind Grace. After the usual questions as to whether she cared for the dancing, he said,—

" My mother was so delighted to get your note. She is glad that Sir Mordaunt and you can dine with us. Have you met Bagshot, our great lawyer and wit? We hope to get him and one or two others to meet you. But it will be quite a small party. You won't mind ? "

" Oh! I shall like it so much better. Every one is most hospitable to us here ; but I prefer small parties to large ones. Mr. Gunning," she called to her host, who was passing, ' do ask Carmencita to sing while she dances. I am told that is the most charming thing she does."

" Why, yes! Michael Angelo Brown will get her. He speaks Spanish, you know, and understands how to tackle her."

He was going, when the princess stopped him.

"And after that, if you can induce her husband to dance with her—he is difficult to persuade, sometimes, but if you can only succeed —it is charming! so *entrain!* And there is something in their being husband and wife so —I don't know what! You understand? Ah!" She heaved a deep sigh.

The young man looked as though he did not in the least ; but he hurried off to find the artist ambassador, who should convey his request to both the performers. And, pleased with the fervour of her reception, the lady consented, so far as she and the song were concerned. It was a long story in couplets, threaded, so to speak, with dances. The precise meaning of each verse required some knowledge of Spanish to understand, but her marvellous play of countenance, and the variety of expression in that low, husky voice, which she *trod* with all the subtlety and delicacy of a great artist, told quite enough. This performance seemed to Grace to be even more remarkable, and certainly more pleasing than the preceding ones. When it was finished, she looked round once more with her bright enthusiasm, to try and

catch Mr. Ferrars' eye, but he was no where in
sight. All she discovered was Mordaunt and
Miss Hurlstone in a distant corner, where she
had seen them more than an hour ago,
engrossed in each other's conversation. Well!
Dear Mordaunt was an out-and-out flirt ; of
course, it meant nothing with *him*. It was to
he hoped the girl was equally case-hardened.

"Do you know, Miss Ballinger," said Caldwell, "I am afraid I like this singing better than
the opera last night. I'm not worthy of that
grand music. It's such an awful row."

"Which you tried to drown with the sound
of your own voice, I daresay," laughed Grace.
"Most people did. Now everyone paid devout
attention to Carmencita. That isn't fair to
poor Wagner, is it ?"

Here Gunning rushed up. "He has caved
in at last ! He has consented to dance with
her—but only after a regular battle. It was
that funny to watch 'em. Their goings on together were like a play, they were, but she
has got round him. I say, Miss Ballinger, I
want to know if you and your brother won't
come out to Tuxedo on Saturday and stay till
Monday, as my guests. It's an awfully jolly

place, and I'll get up a nice party—just the right set, you know—no outsiders—if you'll come."

"You are very good; but it is impossible. We are engaged."

"What? both days? Couldn't you come for one?"

"No. *I*, at least, am engaged both days. I can't answer for my brother."

And so, after the little dramatic dance of coquetry, and pursuit and capture between the Spanish husband and wife was gone through, the evening came to an end.

CHAPTER VIII.

THE next morning, Grace sat turning over the leaves of a book which had just been sent her. The elderly author had been presented to her the evening before, and had promptly sent her his " Souvenirs," which were said to be having a great sale, especially in the Far West, where its axioms of etiquette and records of high life in New York were accepted with unquestioning reverence. A smile played on the girl's face, culminating now and again in a burst of merriment, as her eye fell on such passages as these :

" It is well to be in with the nobs who are born to their position ; but the support of the swells is more advantageous, for society is sustained and carried on by the swells ! "

Grace fairly screamed when she read of some man who was supposed to have been in fashionable English life, that " He was *in* with all the

K 2

sporting world—intimate with the *Champion Prize-fighter, the Queen's Pages, Tattersall's and others !*"

She had just come to this passage when there was a knock at her door, and in response to her "Come!" (in America the invitation is confined to that monosyllable), Mr. Ferrars was announced.

"Why did you disappear so suddenly last night?" asked Grace, with her usual indiscreet directness, as soon as they had shaken hands. "I don't believe you heard Carmencita sing, after all?"

"No, I did not. There was someone there I did not wish to meet. I had to go. I told you New York society and I would never agree. It proved so last night. I shall not try the experiment again. I shall leave New York to-morrow."

"Is it not a pity to take life so very hard as you do?"

"It is life that took *me*."

"You strike me as treading very heavily on it. "'Glissez, et n'appuyez pas,' is such a wise motto."

"I see you have Golightly's 'Souvenirs,'"

he pointed to the book on her lap. " Perhaps you are right. I suppose the career of that veteran butterfly proves it. I suppose, if I had been born like him, I should be happier than I am."

Grace opened the book, and read this passage aloud :

" If you see a fossil of a man, shabbily dressed, it is better to cross the street, and avoid meeting him."

" There is a fitness in such noble sentiments being expressed in this refined language ! I fancy I hear you saying that."

He shrugged his shoulders.

" Golightly is the natural outcome of a society that is built solely upon wealth. I look upon that rubbish as the most salutary lesson our people could have of the depth of degradation to which a 'leader of society,' as he is called, may sink."

" Oh ! but he is a joke, you know ; ask any .one. It is absurd to judge a whole community by one foolish man."

" I am glad you find the society to your taste," he returned drily. " By-the-bye, I have heard from Mrs. Courtly to-day. She asks if

I know when you are likely to be in Boston, and will pay her a visit at her country place, Brackly."

"Mordaunt has made no plans for leaving New York at present. How long do you stay in Virginia?"

"I don't know. It depends; I shall not return to New York; but I *shall* return East shortly, and hope to be with Mrs. Courtly at the same time you are."

"I shall be very glad if you are." Then she added, with a smile, "You will not object to Boston Society?"

"No, I shall not. Mrs. Courtly does not suffer fools gladly. You will not be dull in her house."

"I am never dull anywhere, certainly not here, where I have found plenty to interest and amuse me. I might say more than this, but I am afraid you would sneer."

"Pray go on. I won't sneer."

"I have found something to respect and to admire, which I do not find at home—in our best society. And that is, a much higher moral standard."

"How so? Not in public affairs? Not in

railways? Not in the Press? Not in Wall
Street?"

"I know nothing about those things. I
speak of what comes under my personal observation. I see that women and even men are
tabooed, about whom there is any open scandal.
It is not so with us. Nothing short of divorce
shuts the door against a woman of position who
sins; and as to a man, nothing except cheating
at cards seems to do so."

He rose, without reply, and went to the
window. At the same moment Mordaunt
entered.

"Good morning, Ferrars. Grace, I have a
note from that good natured chap, Gunning,
enclosing a box for the Circus, this afternoon.
Will you come?"

"Is the box our very own, or is Mr. Gunning
coming with friends?"

"He says he may drop in—but the box is
ours, to fill as we like, only it's rather late to
get any one."

"Will you come, Mr. Ferrars? and I will
telephone to ask Mrs. Caldwell and her
daughter."

Ferrars accepted; and so, a few minutes

later, did the ladies. Soon after two o'clock,
the whole party, except Gunning, was established in the great arena to witness Barnum's
show of " Nero." The vast building was
crowded. Grace, who now met the Caldwell
ladies for the first time, was charmed with
them. The mother's sweet, frank face, and
the young girl's freshness and intelligence—an
intelligence very different from " the needle-like
sharpness which pricked and startled one," as
Grace described it, in May Clayton, she was
equally delighted with both. Doreen Caldwell
was not yet seventeen. She gave the promise
of being a very pretty woman ; at present she
was too thin, her face too narrow, and her eyes
unduly large for the rest of the features. She
was strangely quiet for an American, almost
shy, but then her bringing up had been different
from that of most of her country-women, without the constant excitement and restlessness
which seem inseparable from a home-education
in most city households. She had an abundance
of the national humour, quick perceptions, and
a keen capacity for enjoyment ; but she had
not as yet, if she ever would acquire, that particular attraction in the eyes of most English-

men, the spontaneous up-bubbling garrulity which most English*women* call "a feverish desire to be prominent."

Mordaunt talked chiefly to the mother, Grace saw at once that the daughter did not particularly attract him ; it was not this that he had come out into the wilderness for to see. Beatrice Hurlstone's undisguised encouragement and capacity for flirtation treated as a Fine Art, or May Clayton's audacious drollery was much more to his taste. But Ferrars and Grace together drew Doreen out, and were entertained with the remarks of this child of nature, as yet unblasée by the glitter of such shows. A young man came in to visit Mrs. Caldwell, whose box he believed it to be. She introduced him to Grace as Mr. Alan Brown. He was evidently intimate with the family. The girl greeted him with a frank smile, and said,—

"I am sure you have never seen anything better than *this* in Europe. Say, have you, now ?"

"No," he answered. "Barnum takes the cake for shows. It isn't a very grand thing to take the cake for—but it's the best we have in the dramatic line."

This remark, and Mr. Brown's "English accent," gave Grace the key-note of the air which persecuted the young man's life. He had been educated at Eton and Oxford, and had returned to business in New York, hating his present existence, and indisposed to find pleasure in the many pleasurable things his native land had to offer him.

" I am sorry for him," said Mrs. Caldwell, when he had left the box. " Alan is a very nice fellow in many ways, but his education has been a mistake. His father is very rich—dry goods, you know—and this is his only son. As he naturally wishes him to continue the business, it was not fair to bring him up with all the tastes and habits of your leisure class in England. It was his mother's fault. He hates business, and he hates New York."

Gunning entered just then, and was presented to Mrs. Caldwell.

"You live near the Rockies, don't you ? I shot six bears there last year. It was great sport. I was under canvas. But to live there—Caldwell must find it awfully slow."

" My son has work there, and he likes the life. He enjoys New York for a short time, but he would soon tire of doing nothing. He told me what a charming party you had last night," she added.

"Why, yes. It was a success, I think—I hope you thought it went off well, Miss Ballinger? Oh! Thank you. It's awfully good of you to say so. Everyone was so delighted to meet you—and Sir Mordaunt. Sorry you can't come to Tuxedo. Quite a number of people are going there on Saturday. You are going to the ball to-night, of course? And have you cards for the Assembly ball next week? That's all right. Talking of cards, I wish you'd tell me which is the correct thing in London, to print your address on the right-hand or the left-hand corner of your card? 'Cause it's important to know."

"I am afraid I can't tell you. I never thought about it."

"Well, now, that's curious. We've had quite a dispute about it here. I say, don't you want to know who is in the third box from here, that handsome woman in grey? She's Otero, the rival of Carmencita, and a sight better-looking too, but she's not the fashion like the other is. Fashion is everything after all, ain't it? This circus is full all the time. Everybody comes here, not that they care for it very much, but it's the thing. Pity it's so big, one can't see across the house well." Here he took up his glass. "Why! I declare there's Miss Planter and her mother! They must have arrived from Pittsburg yesterday. If I'd known it, I'd have asked her last night. Didn't you meet her in London? Why! she made quite a stir there—went into first-rate society and refused a lord, I am told. You must be introduced, Sir Mordaunt. She is a real belle, Clare Planter is. If you like to come right away now, I'll present you."

So Ballinger rose laughing, and the young men left the box. On his return, just before the end of the performance, Mordaunt reported that the young lady was charming, the prettiest girl he had seen since he landed, lots to say for herself, and very nice. " A sort of girl you'll like, Grace. Been in England too."

Grace knew what that meant. They trooped out of the theatre, Grace on Gunning's arm, Mrs. Caldwell on Sir Mordaunt's. Doreen had a double bodyguard; Ferrars, whose arm she took on one side, and Alan Brown, who had ap-

peared again just as they were leaving, on the
other. As they reached the crowded entrance
Grace saw a sallow foreigner in front of them,
with a lady on his arm. The lady turned her
head, the face was an unforgetable one ; it was
that of Madame Moretto. There was a block
at the door of people waiting for their carriages,
for it was raining.

"Where is Doreen ? I do not see her,"
said Mrs. Caldwell ; but a moment later the
girl appeared on Mr. Brown's arm. Then,
"What have you done with Mr. Ferrars ? I
thought you were with him ? "

"So I was, mother, but he suddenly dropped
my arm, and asked me to excuse him, and let
Alan take me to the carriage. He looked so
odd, quite ill, I thought."

"Certainly Mr. Ferrars is not fit for New
York society," thought Grace to herself. "I
don't believe he was ill a bit. It was one of his
strange vagaries."

The ball that night at one of the greatest
and most exclusive houses in New York will be
best described in an extract from Grace's
letter to her aunt, written the following day.
It tells better than I could the fresh impres-

sions made upon her receptive nature by the
scene, the habits, and the actors in that drama
of the New World in which she was now taking
part.

" *Thursday, January 24th.*

" We were last night at Mrs. Thorly's ball.
Everything was very splendid, the house, the
dresses, the diamonds, the flowers, everything
except the introduction to the fête, by which I
mean that the guests, on arrival, had to
struggle through the brilliant crowd in order to
reach the staircase, and up to the cloak room
on the first floor. This strange anomaly, I am
told, is almost universal here. It was snowing,
and everyone wore " gums," to protect their
thin shoes. The men were naturally muffled in
ulsters ; the women swathed in veils and fur
cloaks. Anything more incongruous than this
unsightly procession forcing its way through the
bare shoulders and wreathed heads of those who
had already discarded their wraps and were
scanning each new arrival, can hardly be imagined. The ordeal of running the gauntlet
through this crowd was most disagreeable to
me. I should not have minded so much if I
had been impenetrably veiled as most of the

women were; but I felt as if the snow-flakes were in my hair, and my cheeks a-flame, as I heard people whisper, " That's the English girl, you know." When I had smoothed my ruffled feathers, I descended with Mordy, and we made our way to Mrs. Thorly, who received me most graciously. As I looked round I was really dazzled by the *general*—more than the particular—beauty of the women, and specially by their toilettes. No one of them, perhaps, was really beautiful ; but they were nearly all pretty, and, as a whole, better dressed than any collection of girls I ever saw. I had on that frock of Mrs. Mason's, which I had only worn once at Grosvenor House; and I flattered myself I looked so smart till I saw how much fresher all the dresses round me were. Well, it didn't much signify. There was a time when I should have been vexed, but now—I don't much care. The married women's diamonds were amazing; many of them wore tiaras, which I understand is an importation from England, much reprehended by some. 'What business have republicans with crowns?' a man said to me. I replied that republicans had taken them off so many heads

that I did not suppose they attached any importance to them as the insignia of royalty. I
preferred walking about and watching the
dancers to dancing much; the young men
were indulgent with me, they showed me
everything, told me who everyone was, and
were very nice and kind. Mordy divided his
attentions between Miss Hurlstone—who is
certainly much taken with him—and a Miss
Planter, a new beauty just arrived. She was
the handsomest girl there, and I admire her
more than anyone I have seen. There is
character in her fine, fearless eyes, her well-
cut mouth, her firm, erect carriage. She is
more like a married woman than a girl, and her
very costly attire strengthened this impression.
Mordy introduced us. Her voice is peculiarly
pleasant, so rich and low, very unlike most of
the voices here. She has a few American
turns of speech (of which she is quite unconscious, of course, for her great desire, I am
told, is to be thought English), but no twang,
not the faintest suspicion of one. She talked
of all the people she had known in London with
a familiarity which was amusing. An English
girl would have made a mess of it; but adapta-

bility is essentially an American feature. She
had fallen into these people's lives, for the time
being, so completely, that she may be said to have
assimilated them. Of course, she is a flirt ; all
girls here are. On the other hand, married
women are *not;* husbands would never stand
their wives "carrying on" as they do all over
the continent of Europe, including England.
We theorize about morality ; but the variable
laws which decree how much people may sin
before they are excluded from society, are much
more lax with us than in New York.

"The supper was most picturesque. At a
given moment any quantity of little tables were
brought in by numberless servants and
scattered through the rooms, and at these the
whole of the guests seated themselves and
were served. The feast lasted quite an hour,
during which there was an entire cessation from
dancing. To me individually this was a trial,
for I had promised Mr. Gunning to go to
supper with him, believing it would be an affair
of ten minutes—I scarcely touch supper, as
you know. Instead of that, I found myself
wedged between him and a man I did not know ;
and Mr. Gunning was absurd enough, and tact-

less enough to choose this moment to propose to me. Can you imagine a more irritating position? No escape. When I declined the honour he did me, hot cutlets were being handed over my shoulder; and there I had to sit while quails, and lobster salads, creams, and ices came in slow succession, and still he poured out his persistent nonsense! I was so angry; I could have boxed his ears.

"*January* 25*th.*—Miss Hurlstone drove me out this morning in her pony-carriage. Of course we discussed the ball, but had not got very far when she turned round and asked if I admired Miss Planter. I replied, 'Yes, very much.' 'So does your brother,' she remarked. Then, after a pause, 'Does he confide in you much?' I was rather taken aback. 'He does sometimes, I suppose, not always.' 'Has he ever spoken to you of me?' 'Yes, two or three times.' 'Do you think he likes me?' 'Certainly; why should he talk to you otherwise? But Mordaunt is a dreadful flirt. You mustn't take anything he says seriously, especially *here*, where he has been told you all expect to be flirted with, and attach no importance to it.' 'Well,' she said, as she flicked

her ponies, 'if he thinks we all take it like
that, he is mistaken—and, I suppose, therefore,
the less I see of him the better, for I never
met anyone I liked so much. That is just the
truth, Miss Ballinger, and, until last night, I
fancied— But when I saw how he was carrying
on with that Planter girl—they are just
nobodies, coals, or tallow, or something from
Pittsburg—I was so hurt, I could have cried.
I suppose you think it very undignified of me
to own it? Mamma would be very angry if
she knew that I said so ; but it is the truth!'
What could I say? I tried to console her by
the assurance that Mordaunt was too *volage* to
settle down with Miss Planter or Miss any one
else just at present, and though I doubt if this
carried much weight with it, the girl's worldly
common sense, so at variance, according to
our ideas, with this expansiveness of sentiment,
stopped her from saying more. I have given
you the dialogue, as nearly as I can, in the
very words used, because its directness—the
way in which she went straight to her point
without hesitation—struck me as very characteristic of the nation. She wanted to learn
something, and she learnt it. Most English

girls would have died sooner than have made
that confession. As to Mordy, of course, none
of these flirtations mean anything; but he will
be burnt some day if he goes on playing with
fire. Miss Planter is really far above the common run. As I looked at Miss Hurlstone's
pretty face, and recalled the other's fine
classical head, I could not be surprised at
Mordy's transference of his admiration. After
all, if American girls choose to flirt in this way,
and encourage men without any intention of
marrying them, they must take the conse-
quences if *they* are sometimes the ones to suffer. I cannot pity Miss Hurlstone very much.
Some of the men here I like greatly. The
women are superior in superficial qualities;
they have more leisure to give to them. But
among the men not devoted solely to money-
making, among those who aim at raising the
intellectual tone of the people, I have met
some well worth cultivating. Mordy's friend,
Mr. Reid, you would like; a shrewd head for
business, with brains to spare for other things.

" But I must stop. Good night. We are
waiting anxiously to hear when you think you
may be able to join us."

CHAPTER IX.

QUINTIN FERRARS was gone; and Miss Ballinger acknowledged to herself that she missed
his visits greatly. His conversation, it is true,
aroused her combativeness as no one else's
did; but then, no one interested and at the
same time puzzled her, as did this strange man.
It cannot be said that she thought much of
him, when alone, for her mind was still engrossed with the image of a very different
person, between whom and herself a gulf, wider
than the Atlantic, had been fixed. But in the
human procession that passed daily before her
eyes, no figure was as vivid as that of Ferrars,
none that she could have missed as she did
his. Under no circumstances could she have
loved this man; his nature was not heroic.
And the only men who had exercised, or could
by any possibility ever exercise, an influence on
her life, had, whether rightly or wrongly, seemed
to her as heroes. For Quintin Ferrars she felt

very sorry, but no respect. His existence appeared to be a wasted one. She admired his intellectual capacity, his very strangeness had a certain attraction for her; the knowledge that there was some real cause for his unhappiness, though she was ignorant of that cause, all made him an interesting person in her eyes. But there her feeling for him stopped. The more she studied his character, the more she felt that there was something which evaded her. He had shirked a duty; he had not fallen in a fair stand-up fight with life—he almost acknowledged as much—and it is not of such stuff that heroes are made.

But Grace Ballinger was a woman, and not above a woman's weaknesses. She liked appreciation—admiration—call it what you will; and, though possessed of no craving to have a man always at her feet, the constant occupation —it might almost be called the devotion—of a clever and original one was certainly agreeable to her. She did not even now realize all that this meant to Ferrars. He sought her as he did no one else; but his reticence as to his own feelings on every personal subject, blinded her to the fact that she was growing to be of paramount importance in his scheme for the future. They had now been nearly a month in New York, and had met almost daily, yet it never occurred to her to regard his assiduity in a very serious light. Her view of it was that he found an intellectual pleasure in her society, nothing more. He was too self-absorbed in brooding over past troubles to feel any longer a passionate interest in any one. Mordaunt, standing further off, discovered what she did not. We cannot see the object accurately that is held too close to our eyes.

And so it came to pass that, when he bade her good-bye with a certain rigidity and difficulty of utterance, she expressed her sorrow at his departure with more than her usual frankness.

" I am so sorry you are going. I hope you will try and be at Brackly when we are there."

" Yes. You may depend on that. Mrs. Courtly will write to me; she has promised."

" I fancy we shall not be there beyond the middle of February, and I think, from what my brother said yesterday, he means to go to Boston straight from here."

Mordaunt had dropped something more than

this, to wit, that Miss Planter was a friend of Mrs. Courtly's, and was going to stay at Brackly in February. But Grace did not give this reason for the faith that was in her as regarded her brother's movements.

" I hope you are going to do your duty as a good American citizen," she said smiling, as she shook his hand.

" I am going to fulfil the law, at all events," he returned grimly. And then he departed.

What an odd man he was, to be sure ! How difficult it was to understand him ! Perhaps the explanation of it was that the lens of his mental photographic apparatus was ill-adjusted: not only were the shadows too black, the objects themselves were distorted ; and the nearer they stood in relation to him, the more they were out of focus.

Mrs. Van Winkle's party that evening was no compromise. She had nailed her colours fast to the staff of fashion : and literature, save in her own fair person, was unrepresented. Mr. Sims, who stood on the borderland of the two worlds, and the young painter, Michael Angelo Brown, at present engaged on a portrait of Mrs. Van Winkle in the character of Diana,

with a crescent on her head and a bow in her
hand,—these were the pinches of salt thrown
in to flavour the social compound, with a
regard to Miss Ballinger's appetite for something stronger than a fashionable *soufflé*. It
is true that bright creature, Mrs. Siebel,
was of the party, whose shrewd perceptions and
ebullient sense of fun irradiated any circle.
But then, in Mrs. Van Winkle's eyes, she was
first of all a woman of fashion ; only a delightful
human being afterwards. For Sir Mordaunt,
Mrs. Van Winkle felt herself to be feast enough ;
but with the happy confidence of a woman who
fears no rivalry, she had selected two pretty
units of the " Four Hundred " to add brilliancy
to the entertainment. She looked unusually
well herself, in pale blue velvet, with powdered
hair and pearls. When Grace remarked how
much they became her, she whispered,—

" Diamonds are getting so vulgar ! Look
at the poor dear Princess. She is always like
a badly-made *blanc-mange*, but to-night she
looks as if she had been upset in a jeweller's
window, and had got mixed up with the
diamonds."

For the Princess Lamperti's ample white

form was resplendent with jewels, two neck-
laces defining a waist which it would have
taken a Life Guardsman to encircle.   Not
wholly unlike a Life Guardsman was Mr. George
Ray, who was on her left, while the host sat
between her and Miss Ballinger.   He was a
well-favoured gentleman of fifty, with extremely good manners, and not much besides.
The dinner was perfect, and the ingenuity with
which it was *coloured* gave rise to some amusement, of the thin, obvious kind which anyone
can enjoy.   The table was covered with forget-
me-not growing out of moss, procured for
Mrs. Van Winkle with infinite difficulty at this
season.   The candle-shades were pale blue ;
the bills of fare were printed, as were the names
of each guest, on pale blue cards.   Of course
the menu began with Blue Point oysters.
Then there was a *Potage à la Mazarin*, having
an occult reference to the tint associated with
the cardinal of that name.   This was followed
by *Truites au bleu*, and what Mrs. Van
Winkle had christened "True-blue Fillets of
Salmon."   After that there came a compote of
"blue-rock pigeons," and I know not what
other birds of the air, and entrées of meat which

had been re-christened for the nonce. In the second course there was a jelly of blueberries, I remember, and finally the menu closed with a *fondu au cordon bleu.*

On the other side of Grace was Mr. Sims. He fired his little shots alternately at the hostess, the Princess, and other ladies across the table, breaking up the *têtes-à-têtes* with the laughter which followed his assaults.

" I never saw so becoming a ' fit of the blues ' as your dress, Mrs. Van Winkle," he declared.

" It is quite too sweet of you to say so ; you don't generally pay compliments."

" He would not have done so now but for the temptation of the pun," laughed Mrs. Siebel. " I wonder he did not get in something about ' blue stockings.' "

" It was an oversight," he replied merrily. " Couldn't you have concocted a dish ' *au bas-bleu*,' Mrs. Van Winkle ? "

" You don't suppose I did not think of it ? My avoidance of that opprobrious term was deliberate. Literary women never understand the art of eating ; I am the exception. With me it is a *fine* art. Observe the combination in this menu. The sequence of flavours is as delicately felt as the juxtaposition of colours on Titian's canvases."

"You mean it is 'a symphony in blue' ? "

" Exactly. You think you are making an epigram, Mr. Sims. You are uttering the simple truth. There are no harsh discords here. You are led up from one dish to another ; you may eat straight through this dinner. You will find that all the surprises *resolve* themselves, like the surprises in harmony."

" Great Scot ! " cried Mr. Sims. " I had no idea eating was allied to music, as well as to painting ! It only remains to drag in Poetry."

" Oh ! " interposed Grace, " she requires no dragging. Does not she step in of her own accord ? From Homer downwards all the grand, healthy old poets take delight in the pleasures of the table. It is only the morbid, attenuated school that feed on rose-leaves."

" That reminds me of the ' Souls,' that exclusive society of æsthetes in London we have heard so much about," said Mrs. Van Winkle. " Are you a ' Soul,' Miss Ballinger ? "

Grace laughed. " I am no*body*, but I am not a ' Soul.' "

" I should like to be one," sighed her hostess. " But must I abandon all the pleasures of the flesh to be admitted to this spiritual community ? "

" No ; some female ' Souls' are very corporeally active—a sort of ' Walkyre'—spirits on horseback. They ride ; they hunt."

" In couples ?" asked the hostess with an air of infantine innocence.

" Only misanthropes like doing things alone," returned Grace, with a smile. " I am sure I don't."

" Nor I !" cried Mrs. Siebel.

" My dear, who is prepared to contradict you ? " Mrs. Van Winkle played with a morsel of jelly on the end of her fork, as she spoke. " We all love humanity too much. Yes, I wish I were a Soul ! "

" Well ! " said Sims, reflectively, with a funny twitch of his mouth, " you fence beautifully, and I have seen you dance a *pas seul*—two recommendations, I believe, to Souldom." Then turning to the large lady, who certainly looked as if she could neither fence nor dance a *pas seul*, he continued : " And you, Princess, what do *you* say ? Do you feel like being a ' Soul' ? "

The Princess paused, and looked grave, before she replied,—

" I don't quite know what it all means, Mr. Sims; but if it has anything to do with ghosts, and visions, and second sight, I have the best right to join the society, for I am very *croyante*. I have had *such* experiences !   Ah ! "

" Do tell us about them."

" A ghost story first hand !   How delightfull ! " said several people round the table.

" Not now, not while we are at table," returned the Princess. "Perhaps by-and-by." . . . And no one had the bad taste to insist further.

But Mrs. Van Winkle who, no matter at what cost, was never content to play second fiddle, here observed,—

" I once saw a ghost—or what I took to be a ghost—in St. Petersburg, in the dusk of the evening, in my room.   I was dreadfully frightened.   It proved to be a Russian ; those foreigners are so very enterprising. He had long shown his admiration. He now sprang at me with a drawn sword in his hand.   Happily, I was near the bell, or it might have been very awkward."

" And what became of the ghost ? " asked

Mordaunt, biting his lips.   " Did you have him
arrested ? "

" Oh, no, I felt too much compassion for
him, poor man !   Indeed, I was very much
touched.   There is so little romance in this
present day."

" What a charming comprehensive word that
is, my dear Mrs Van Winkle ! " laughed Sims.
"It includes murder, highway robbery, and
now, I see, other little offences ! "

A good deal of amusement was caused by
this peculiar revelation, and one can only
imagine the narrator intended that such should
be the result.   I am confident she rarely expected to be taken seriously.   If she could
shock or astonish her audience by her utterances she was satisfied.   She had certainly
driven the ghosts from the field.

But when dinner was over, and the men had
rejoined the ladies in that bower of em-
broideries and perfume where Mrs. Van Winkle
received her guests, lapped in langorous repose
on satin cushions, and no one's face could be
distinguished under the dim irreligious light of
silk-shrouded lamps, then the narrator of abnor-
mal experiences being pressed by her hostess,

began, without reluctance, without a shadow of hesitation,—

"It will be five years ago next May, I was in Rome and alone. The Prince had left me to go to Palermo, on business, as he said. I had only been married three years, at this time, and though I cannot say I was happy, no! I still loved my husband; I was not completely *desillusionnée*. I knew he was *volage*, but I had no reason to suspect that he was quite—how do you say? estranged from me. I gave him a liberal allowance, over and above what had been settled on him at our marriage, and he always treated me with, well—with respect. He was not *passionné*, no, but I thought, *enfin*, I thought it was not his nature. Well! he went to Palermo, and I had a letter from him in the course of a few days, saying his business was advancing favourably, though slowly. He would probably be detained longer than he expected. I was not anxious, I was not uneasy about him, —why should I be? when I went to bed that night. That made my dream the more extraordinary, *tout à fait saisissante*. I saw him in a garden, under a tree. Beside him stood a dark woman, whose face was quite distinct,

I could have drawn it. She gave him some fruit."

"Were they in the condition of Adam and Eve?" murmured Mrs. Van Winkle, from her pile of satin cushions.

"Oh, no," continued the Princess gravely, "she had a yellow gown on, trimmed with *broderie Anglaise*. I can see it now! He was dressed in grey tweed. He ate the fruit she gave him, and then gradually, gradually, I saw his face change colour, and the expression, ah! *il avait un air méchant*. I had never seen him look like that before—he was almost green—his features hideously distorted. He fell down at her feet, and I knew that she had poisoned him. I woke with a scream!"

"No wonder. You must yourself have eaten something that disagreed with you, Princess!" said Sims.

She shook her head. "No, but my dream disagreed with me! Ah! I was quite *boulversée*, I could not sleep again, and still I saw them distinctly before me. In the morning I rang for my maid, and said I would start for Palermo. My family tried to dissuade me from following my husband, but I said I knew

some misfortune had happened to him, or
would happen, if I did not go. What I had
dreamt was a *presentiment ;* and so persuaded of
this was I, that when I reached Naples, though
a great hurricance was blowing, and I am a
dreadful sailor (*je souffre horriblement*), I insisted on embarking. They told me the steamer
was a very bad one, and really not fit to put to
sea in such weather, but I was firm. *Que
voulez vous?* I was possessed with the idea.
We had a terrible passage, but at last we
reached Palermo, and I drove to the Hotel des
Palmes. I was dreadfully nervous ; I scarcely
dared ask after my husband,'but they told me
he was quite well—he was in the garden—so I
followed him. I could not rest till I had seen,
with my own eyes, that he did not look as he
had done in my dream. I found him under a
tree, a palm tree, in his grey tweed suit, seated
beside a brunette, dressed in yellow; that
Madame Moretto, *who has poisoned his life ever
since !*"

"And does that account for his looking as
he does—so very unwholesome, Princess?"
asked Mrs. Van Winkle.

"Ah! I saw a change in that minute, when

he looked up and perceived me—ah ! he turned
green just as I had seen him in my dream—
d'un ton verdâtre, and his expression, it
was terrible ! That was the beginning of all
my trouble, which lasted nearly five years,
before I consented to divorce him.[1] Have I
not reason, *ma chère*, to believe in spiritual
warnings—second sight, and—and so on ?"

Of course everyone declared that it was a
most interesting and remarkable instance of
spiritual premonition that he or she had ever
heard, direct from the fountain-head. Only
Mr. Sims made a captious remark, to the
effect that the vision seemed to have been
quite useless ; it had resulted in the princess
being very seasick, and very unhappy some
time before she need have been : otherwise, the
warning had produced no effect—one way or the
other.

Grace listened to all this in silence. It was
amazing to her that anyone could bring herself
to relate deliberately so painful an episode in
her past, to hand it over, as it were, for

---

[1] He went to live in Paris, and, having no Italian
property, became a French subject, which enabled her to
do so.

analysis to a cold and curious circle, eager indeed for "some new thing," but not even pretending to feel any warm sympathy for the lady's domestic woes. It confirmed Grace in the opinion that those woes could not be very deep-seated. No doubt this soft feather-bed of a woman had suffered to some extent, but not to the extent which she herself believed ; not as a proud, passionate, sensitive nature would have suffered in like circumstances. To such an one it would have been impossible to make them the subject of after-dinner discussion, in a circle of the merest acquaintance.

She was at some distance from the Princess, and Madame Siebel, who sat near her, whispered,—

"You can take a horse to the water, but you can't make him drink. He was dead sick of his wife five years ago, so she would have done better to set him free then."

"In England we don't think that sort of millstone should be so easily slipped off the neck," returned Grace half seriously, and half playfully. "She has only just divorced him, then ?"

"Only just. He is waiting now, I believe,

for Madame Moretto to divorce *her* husband in order to marry her."

" Good gracious ! Has *she* got a husband also ? And what is the plea in *her* case ? or is it the husband who divorces *her* ? "

" No. He is passive, I am told, in the matter. She pleads desertion, though of course that is all nonsense, for she is ever so rich, and left him years ago. The curious thing is, no one knew she had a husband until the Prince was free to marry her. Then it came out she had been clandestinely married to some American, who had separated from her when he discovered the sort of woman she was."

" Well ! I must say these divorces by mutual consent seem very easily obtained in your country."

" Yes, if you are in the right State, I don't mean state of mind or body, I mean if you go and live for six months in a State where it is the law. Madame Moretto has come over here expressly for that purpose, and is living in Rhode Island, I am told, where divorce is made easy. It is not so in New York."

" But I have seen her here twice ? "

"Oh ! they have only been over for the day. It is a funny story, isn't it ? This sort of double game of chess. To make it complete the American ought now to marry the Princess."

"I should think she had had enough of matrimony.'

"Oh, dear no. She is just the woman to marry again. A husband is a luxury that sort of woman cannot forego. I shouldn't wonder if George Ray the Third were the fortunate man."

"That young Adonis ? Do you mean that he—? Oh ! impossible ! "

"Impossible that he should propose ? Not at all. He is awfully hard up. The only gold, I believe, he possesses is in his teeth." Here she laughed merrily. "Sometimes I think we take a pride in the amount of gold we stuff into our mouths. Talk about the gold-fields, I will back a fashionable churchyard to beat them, as a mine of wealth."

Grace could not help laughing.

"I heard of a man who had a front tooth stuffed with a diamond, but I didn't believe it."

"Why not ? Young men addicted to precious stones have so few opportunities of displaying them. If George Ray the Third marries the Princess, I'll suggest to him that he should wear one of hers, instead of that lump of gold in his eye tooth."

The Princess here rose. It was time to go to the assembly, of which she was a patroness, and whither nearly all the party present were bound.

CHAPTER X.

MORDAUNT BALLINGER'S luncheons at the
"Lawyers' Club," and his introductions to
various magnates of the money-market had
led to his mind being tossed and buffeted on
a sea of railroads, and mines, and joint-stock
companies, until it had settled—as much from
exhaustion, perhaps, as anything—on "real
estate" in one of the rapidly rising cities of
the Far West. This seemed as safe an investment, to bring in a large return for his money,
as he could find. He felt sure Mrs. Frampton
would think so. Still, as his aunt, whose
acuteness in money matters he regarded with
an almost superstitious trust, not wholly un-
mixed with dread, was to join them in the
course of a few weeks, the young man resolved
to defer the purchase of the shares offered him
until he could visit Pueblo, and investigate on
the spot the condition and prospects of the
estate in question.

He came into his sister's room, a morning or two after the Van Winkle dinner, holding an open letter in his hand.

" I've heard from Aunt Su. She has got my letter, and seems in an awful stew about my investing money here. Well, I wrote yesterday to tell her I should do nothing till she came. She thinks she can sail the middle of February, and join us in Boston. By-the-bye, have you written to Mrs. Courtly ? "

" No. I was waiting for you to tell me what time to propose to go to her. I suppose we shall only be there a few days before we go to Boston ? "

" Well, that depends. I believe the Planters are going to her next week. We may as well offer ourselves at the same time."

Grace smiled.

" Certainly." Then, with a malicious glance into her brother's face : " Perhaps Mrs. Courtly would invite Miss Hurlstone, too, if I mentioned her. They are friends, I know."

" Well, don't mention her, then. She is a very nice girl, and all that, but—I'd rather she didn't come."

He stood near the table where his sister was

writing as he said this. Then he took up a pen, and flung it down, fidgetted first on one leg, then on the other, finally walked to the window, still with Mrs. Frampton's letter in his hand, and remained there silent, with his back to Grace for several minutes. She knew him too well not to see there was something on his mind—something which he desired to say to her, and yet found it difficult to express. She thought, not without a twinge of apprehension, of the various ladies to whom he had paid attention here. Could it be that he had entangled himself, more or less, with one of these? Her mind so little anticipated what was coming that she started and flushed when he said,—

" There's something else in Aunt Su's letter which I think you ought to know, Grace. In fact, she says I'm to tell you. Because you're sure to hear of it sooner or later. People are full of it. There's fresh evidence against Lawrence."

Her face hardened. She closed her lips tight for a moment, and in her clear blue eyes there was a momentary flash, as she said quickly,—

" What is it?"

"They've found the draft of another will, dated some years back, by which his uncle left the bulk of his fortune to his other nephew, Giles Tracy, and only 10,000l. to Ivor Lawrence."

"You call that evidence against him? What does that prove?" she asked hotly.

"It only proves that before Ivor got the influence over his uncle which he exercised latterly, the old chap meant to leave his estates, not to his sister's son, but to his brother's son, as was natural, and as it was understood he would do."

"Understood by whom? By Mr. Giles Tracy, I suppose, who took to gambling on the strength of this prospective fortune! And why was it 'natural,' pray, that a man who had made—not inherited—his large fortune, like old Mr. Tracy, should leave it to a spendthrift, a vautrien, instead of to a clever, rising barrister like his other nephew, whose character was universally respected?"

"Well, it isn't universally respected now, Grace."

"The more shame for those who are ready to believe any foul accusation on such evidence!" Her cheeks were aflame, and her voice shook as she spoke. " Evidence ? It is too childish to call this evidence. According to your own showing, all it proves is that the old man once—before he knew how young Tracy would turn out—meant to make him his heir. He discovered in time the comparative worth of both his nephews."

"You forget there is a lot of cumulative evidence against Ivor before; his bringing a lawyer (who happens to have died since) to his uncle's bedside when he was dying—young Tracy's being refused admittance to his uncle—"

" Because the old man could not endure the sight of him latterly. Everyone knows that he refused repeatedly to see him ; and those who had heard him speak of his nephew during the last year or two, were amazed to find that he had left him even so much as 20,000*l.*"

Mordaunt shrugged his shoulders.

" The signature of the will is disputed, as you know."

An ejaculation indicative of intense scorn burst from his sister's lips.

"So he is to be accused of forgery. I

wonder they don't add murder to the charge !
Has the trial begun ?"

" No, it has been again deferred."

She was silent for a moment, leaning her
head upon her left hand, while with a pen in
the right she traced some scrolls upon the note-
paper before her.

" Poor Mr. Lawrence ! " she said, at last. " I
have a great mind to write to him."

" Good God ! You wouldn't dream of doing
anything so undignified, so outrageous, after
his behaviour to you, Grace ? A fellow who
runs after you for months so that half the
world believes you are engaged to him, and
that he is only waiting till he is rich enough to
marry, and who, when he inherits this big
fortune, turns his back and never comes near
you again ; and you would actually demean
yourself to write to him ? "

Strange to say, now that the discussion had
entered upon personal grounds, the young lady
had comparatively regained her composure.
Still it was not without an effort that she said,—

" Mr. Lawrence and I are very good friends,
and I hope we shall always remain so. We
never have been, and, of course, never shall be,

anything more.   I see no reason why I should
not write and assure him that there is one
person who believes in him, if all the verdicts in
the world went against him,—if the whole of
London cut him dead, it would make no
difference to me.   I know him to be a perfectly
honourable, truthful, noble character.   He is
peculiar; there are some very rugged knots in
him which you and Aunt Su, particularly Aunt
Su, could never understand.   And you don't
understand him now.   You think, supposing
that he cared for me, which of course he never
did, that he should have proposed when he
found himself with 10,000*l.* a year.   That is
the last thing he would do with this accusation,
this cloud over his head.   He might have done
so as a poor barrister, but never as one whose
good name was tainted.   I don't say he is right
in avoiding us as he has done ; I think, on the
contrary, he is quite wrong.   But I should not
be afraid of his misunderstanding me if I wrote
to him.   I think he would do justice to my
motives, and thank me."

" All the same, Grace, I do hope to goodness, you won't.   Men of the world are not used
to such high-flown sentiments.   And it's so

very like throwing yourself at the head of a
cad, who—"

" None of that, Mordy, please, or I must ask
you to leave the room." She spoke now with
more excitement. " We have gone through all
the string of opprobrious epithets at your
command before, you know. They produce no
effect on me—yes, they do. They make me
feel very irritable with you. So, like a dear,
drop it, please, and if you mention Mr. Lawrence—I have no objection whatever to your
mentioning him—do so respectfully, as my
friend."

He felt there was nothing more to be said.
He had expended all his ammunition, retreat
alone remained for him. But when the door
was closed behind her brother, the girl's fortitude
and pride broke down. She laid her head
between her hands and the hot tears of wounded
love and disappointment coursed down her
cheeks, and fell on the note-paper upon which
her pen had traced a confusion of curves and
circles. Why had he not spoken to her when
he was a struggling barrister ? Was it because
of her aunt, her brother ? Was it by reason of
false pride ? That he had pride, of an un-

reasoning, indomitable kind, allied to the
obstinacy which was so marked a feature of
his character, she knew well. But this should
not have been enough to have kept him silent
if he cared for her. And unless she was
utterly blinded by vanity, by a fatuous mis-
apprehension of looks she had now and again
found fastened upon her, of casual words and
actions escaping from a reticent man, he had
cared for her at that time. She would sooner
have died than admit to her brother that she believed this. To him, as to her aunt, while hotly
defending Ivor Lawrence, whenever a discussion
concerning him arose, she always declared that
as "there had been nothing between them," her
only feeling as to his now holding aloof from them
was grief at the alienation of the most trusted
friend she had ever had. Of course Mrs.
Frampton was much too acute to be deceived
by these protestations. When the accusations
against Lawrence were made public, Grace's
health and spirits were so visibly affected for a
time that those who loved her most could not
but see how strong a hold this man had taken
on her heart. Nearly eight months had passed
since then, and to all outward seeming she had

recovered her buoyant tone, her healthy interest and capacity of deriving pleasure from things around her. Only at rare moments, and when alone, as now, did the flood-gates of a grief, the well-springs of which lay so far below the surface, rise up and overflow.

Nevertheless, after a while her brave spirit rose. She must not succumb to her trouble. For the sake of others she must put it away from her; she rose and bathed her eyes. She had an engagement to a "ladies' luncheon" party, convened at the house of an agreeable woman, almost a stranger to Grace, who, after securing her, had invited seventeen others "to meet Miss Ballinger." The luncheon was exquisite and well-served; the conversation general and very pleasant.

"I had no idea it could have been *so* pleasant," she said afterwards. "I really think eighteen Englishwomen would have been very dull, all the waves floundering together without a male rock to dash themselves against. But these waves had so much salt in them! I felt myself quite invigorated by plunging among them."

The truth was these waves were rather stronger than those which played, as a rule,

upon the fine shores of fashionable New York
life. The women here met were almost all
interested, and active in better things than
gossip, parties, dress. Their fields and their
aims were diverse; some of them were young
and active, some past middle age, but with keen
intelligence undimmed, sympathies warm as in
girlhood, and a playful humour, a humour
altogether national, conveyed sometimes in a
word, the turn of a phrase, lighting with the
illusive flame of a will-o'-the-wisp swamps into
which an interchange of talk so often flounders.
They were not pretentious, though many of
them did adventure upon subjects that demand
more time, thought, and preparation than most
Englishwomen conceive it fitting to give to
any study. One girl had been through a
course of anatomy; not as it appeared, with
any ulterior object, but in order to master the
wonderful mechanism of the human frame,
"which," as she said, with a hard directness,
which sounded odd in one so young, "being a
fact always present, should interest us more
than it does. We can learn, and we ought to
know all about it; for this is a thing which
affects our whole being here, our present and

our future; whereas our soul, which people trouble themselves so much about, is only a matter of speculation. It seems a pity to waste time on a subject we know so little of."

Grace was too wise to enter into a discussion with the youthful philosopher; this was a phase which would probably pass away in a few years, when, if the girl fell under right influence, she might learn that there were higher truths than those which can be tangibly felt; in the meantime, the uncompromising antagonism to all conventional acceptances, and polite euphemisms, the resolve to seize the truth to her hand, and probe it thoroughly, interested Grace. This was a type of American character she had not yet met.

But among the middle-aged women was one whose studies and experience were far more curious. She had large means, which she had partly expended among the fast diminishing tribe of Zuni Indians in Arizona, whose language she had rescued from oblivion by means of the phonograph. The music of their hymns and chants and invocations for rain had also thus been noted down, and several unique

N 2

objects—notably, a jewelled toad, supposed to
be a god—secured by her excavations. The
ruined city made of adobe, in which this tribe
dwelt, had been saved from total destruction
through this lady's exertions, who induced the
Government to aid her in protecting them from
the attacks of other and more powerful tribes.
So interested had she become in this people,
that she had bidden some of their high-priests
to journey to the East, and visit her—which
they did. She described most graphically their
dignity, their admirable breeding, the eloquence
of their gestures, expressing their meaning so
clearly as scarcely to need the interpreter's
verbal translation of their speech. They went
thrice a day down to the seashore—the house
stood on a cliff—to make their prayers and
libations. "You are not as religious as we
are," they said, "but we suppose you are as
religious as you have time to be."

Some day a learned monograph will be pub-
lished of this people, their language, their faith,
their customs; and the philologists will fight
over their origin, and the plough of civilization
will pass over their poor mud-built city; but
Grace was interested in meeting the enthusiast

through whose courage, energy and devotion so much had been rescued as a text book for historical research. It was a fine sonorous note in the diapason of American character, and the young Englishwoman heard it with pleasure.

That evening she and her brother dined with Mrs. Caldwell. It was not a large party ; and the guests, with the exception of Mrs. Flyn and her sister, were all men—mostly men distinguished in some way other than that of having amassed large fortunes !

It is true that Alan Brown, the young Anglomaniac—"and stupid at that," as May Clayton said—was present, but as he sat next Doreen, to whom he talked in a low tone, his insignificance was not offensive. Brilliant Chudleigh, the advocate, whose scathing eloquence was a proverb, jovial Dr. Parr, simmering with fun, ready to boil over at any moment, wise and witty General Stout, famous in the war, and now in peace time as great a favourite with women as with men, the poet Sloper, so gently humorous, so blandly pungent, Mordaunt's shrewd friend Reid, and two others, whom the Ballingers had not met before, threw in their separate contributions into the common pool,

and produced that best of round games—
general conversation. No one monopolized
the talk, but the men had the best of it.
May Clayton held her own, it is true ; the pro-
vocation of her nimble tongue stimulated the
clever elders around ; her sallies elicited peals
of laughter ; and from time to time, when there
was a lull, she set the humming-top—as with a
neat flick of the whip—once more frantically
spinning. But as dinner progressed, and the
conversation, leaving generalities, entered into
the arena of personal chaff, the spur of the girl's
tongue was not needed. The combatants were
on their mettle, with a gallery to applaud their
brilliant attacks and retorts, their assaults, and
reprises, and carrying of the war into the
enemy's country, each man had his bout ; and
the fooling, conducted with perfect good
humour, was delightful. Such a contest would
not be possible in England. In chaff, we hold
that all is permissible, but the truth. But here
to wound one of these dexterous knights, armed
cap-à-pie, seemed impossible. Chudleigh had
tried for the Presidency of the United States,
and had failed. The mock commiseration he
met with at the hands of Parr, who deplored the

waste of fine oratory spilt upon that occasion, was countervailed by the satirical sympathy Chudleigh affected in rounded periods, at the charges of bribery and corruption brought in the public prints against a well-known body, of which the M.D. was a leading member. This spear-thrust might have been expected to pierce his armour. Not at all; he rode on laughing, and apparently untouched. Then it was proposed that Government should be memorialized to create the post of Laureate to the United States, in order that the poet Sloper should be elected thereto. His verses had failed to soften the hearts of his native town so far as to induce them to send him as their representative to Congress, but this want of appreciation, this deadness of heart—said General Stout, warming to his subject—would, no doubt, disappear when Sloper's Sonnets received the stamp of official recognition. As to the General himself, he received thrusts on all sides, as to his campaigns in stage-land, his conquests in the green-room, his capitulations under (scenic) canvas, his ready response to the cry from oppressed damsels of " Stout to the rescue ! "

The Ballingers were both much amused.

Mordaunt, between Mrs. Caldwell and Mrs.
Flynn, had two foot-notes, as it were, to the
text of all this personal raillery. Mrs. Flynn
was the more ample and unrestrained expositor
of the two : Mrs. Caldwell not going beyond a
hint, sometimes, where the younger and livelier
lady became exhaustive. Grace had Pierce
Caldwell beside her. He fully entered into the
fun, and told her enough to make her understand the point of each attack, the dexterity of
each defence, the imperturbable good temper
with which all who mingled in the fray bore the
several blows.

"People say you Americans are thin-skinned,"
she said. "Perhaps there is one side of you—
that side which you turn to *us*, which has a sensitive skin ; but the other side, that which is
presented to yourselves, must be covered with
a perfect hide ! Englishmen could no more
stand these blows below the belt, they would
turn very nasty. I saw a clever young man
once in a country house retire to bed, because
—we were playing at ' Twenty-one Questions '
—he was so offended at an impudent bit of
chaff. We had thought of the Duke of Wellington's Monument in St. Paul's, and when he

could not guess it, and had to be told, he declared indignantly he had never heard of it. 'Perhaps you never heard of the Duke of Wellington,' said a pert prig; whereupon the discomfited guesser went straight off to bed. Now, I see that no American could possibly be so silly. You have your tempers so admirably in hand."

"Well, I don't know about that," said Pierce dubiously. "It all depends on whether we think a man means mischief or not. These fellows here, you see, are all good friends. They enjoy sharpening their wits on each other."

"So it seems," said Grace, laughing.

Dr. Parr, on her other side, had been watching his opportunity to fire sly shots obliquely across the table at Chudleigh, and had not heard the foregoing. He now turned round and addressed the young Englishwoman with the unmistakable air that says, "Enough of fooling. Let us be serious," though there was still a sub-cutaneous twitch about his mouth.

"What do you think of us, Miss Ballinger? I am afraid you will go back and say we are an *un*licensed set of victualers, making a terrible row, without any manners, any polish, eh ?"

" I am so glad you put it that way, instead of asking me what I think of America, which is so difficult to answer, and which I am asked, upon an average, twelve times every day. It isn't at all difficult to answer *you*. I should like to dine with such unlicensed victuallers every day of my life."

" Great Scot ! This is, indeed, an incentive to continue in our evil ways," cried the doctor. "You cannot be English, Miss Ballinger, quite, *quite* English ? A drop of Irish or Foreign must be infused into your blue blood, surely ? "

" Why so ? Are we not the most appreciative nation upon earth ? "

" Critical—say critical—and I am with you. You measure everything by one standard—your own. I don't say you are wrong, but it makes English approval sometimes appear to be tinged with—what shall I say ? condescension ? Do you know the story of the American who drew the attention of a patriotic Briton to a gorgeous sunset here ? The Britisher replied, " Sunset ? Ah ! you should see one of Her Majesty's sunsets ! "

Grace laughed heartily.

"That is very cruel of you, Dr. Parr. I wanted to say such a number of nice things to you, and now I can't. I shall have to pour them all out to Mr. Chudleigh, who won't call my appreciation, 'condescension.'"

Here a name, bandied across the table, struck Grace's ear.

"Planter has cornered the market, they say."

"He has high Scriptural authority for doing so," said Chudleigh. "Joseph cornered the market, and made a very good thing out of it."

"I suspect that is more than Planter will do," struck in the General. "He will come to grief some day with his gigantic speculations."

"What!" cried May Clayton, with her chirruping little voice, "has he bitten off more than he can chew?"

Ballinger laughed immoderately. Probably this turned Miss Clayton's attention more directly to him.

"By-the-bye, Sir Mordaunt, is it true that you are going to give up your baronetcy, and become an American citizen?"

"You have given me too little encouragement," he replied promptly, with a stage
sigh.

"Well!" she said, "I don't know about
encouragement. I should say you have
neglected your opportunities. But I believe
you followed my advice. Only take care you
don't bark up the wrong tree."

"There's such a forest," he said. "It's awfully
confusing."

Grace had some conversation with her hostess
after dinner.

The Caldwells were to leave New York for
their home in the Rocky Mountains in the
course of a week. It was arranged that Grace
should write to Mrs. Caldwell when she and
her brother went Westward, and Mrs. Frampton
was included in the cordial invitation to
"Falcon's Nest," offered to the English
travellers.

"I like Mrs. Caldwell," said Mordaunt as
they drove home. "She is a good sort. The
girl's dull."

"Not at all, she is young, and has not lost
the sweet privileges of youth for remaining in
the background, as Miss Clayton has."

"Give me a girl who has lost the privilege,
then. I can't stand a bread-and-butter miss.
I wish Mrs. Caldwell would ask Mrs. Flyn and
her cousin to Falcon's Nest when we are there ;
not that I shall be there for more than a day
or two, I fancy. I shall leave you and Aunt
Su, while I go off to Pueblo, and stay with
Charington at his ranche."

" I should not much like to be shut up with
Aunt Su and Miss Clayton," returned his sister,
laughing. " It would be what you call ' rather
warm quarters.' I like the girl myself. I am
sure there is no harm in her—not half so much
as there is in many very demure girls—but I
fancy I see Aunt Su's face at her way of going
on ? I shouldn't mind her meeting Miss
Planter now," she added, glancing with a smile
at him as the lamplight flashed upon his face.
" Miss Planter would not offend her taste."

He did not reply, and the rest of the drive
home was performed in silence.

CHAPTER XI.

THE ball of hospitality which had been set rolling by kindly hands a month since, was snatched from one to another, during that last week of our travellers' stay in New York, and seemed to acquire a more vigorous impetus as the day of their departure drew near. That this constant round of social engagements was fatiguing to Grace, that she longed for a little repose, and leisure for reflection, is true ; but, under the circumstances, perhaps it was as well that this luxury was withheld. She had come abroad, as her brother's companion, with the definite resolve to put the past behind her. For months one subject—one cruel, gnawing trouble—had absorbed all her thoughts. It should do so no longer. She would never suffer a hint of reproach, or a word of accusation against Ivor Laurence to fall from the lips of either her aunt or brother, without defending him hotly. But, unless forced to do so, she never uttered his name. Both Mrs. Frampton and Mordaunt recognized the effort to dismiss him from her heart. They thought they were help- ing her to do so ; but they learnt the inefficacy of abuse. Happily, there was a natural rebound in her healthy temperament against sitting down with folded hands, and doing nothing in this world. Visiting the poor was not in her line ; she had tried " slumming " in London, and had found it a failure ; it was the only thing which paralyzed her with shyness. The pursuit of science and art were equally foreign to her nature. The work which seemed fitting and natural for her just now was to be Mordaunt's help-mate and companion, until such time as he should select one for life. He was not made to be alone. And this work which her hand had found, she would do, as she had done everything, with all her might.

Therefore it was that she had thrown herself frankly and without stint into the stream of society in New York, resolved to take what interest and amusement she could find, without letting anyone—least of all her brother—see the dark shadow that obtruded itself, from time

to time, across the brilliant scene. And she
had her reward. There is not so much cordiality in the world that a warm-hearted girl
can remain indifferent to such a welcome as had
been accorded to Grace, even where there was
not much in common between her and her new
acquaintances. Some she really liked greatly;
some had only amused her; towards all she
felt unaffectedly grateful for the many thoughtful attentions she had received. The Hurlstones
had been persistently kind, and now proposed
to receive Mrs. Frampton, their old acquaintance, on her landing; but, as regarded them,
Grace could not but feel it was just as well
that her brother and she were leaving New
York. If the girl took Mordaunt's spasmodic
flirtation seriously, the sooner he was removed
from her the better. Grace was sceptical as to
his ever being very hard hit; at all events
Beatrice Hurlstone was not the one to deal the
decisive blow.

As to her other acquaintances, the Caldwells
and Mrs. Siebel were those from whom she
parted with most regret. The first Grace
hoped soon to see again; the latter was to be
in Europe next summer, when she and Miss

Ballinger would meet. Jem Gunning had gone to recover his equilibrium from defeat at St. Augustine. Grace was glad to be spared any farewells from the young millionaire. Mr. Sims was so peripatetic that he might turn up anywhere, at Boston, or Chicago, or San Francisco. " As long as I am this side the grave you are never safe from me," as he himself put it. Mrs. Van Winkle proposed to give a *Thé Funèbre* on the Ballingers' departure. She had lately given one, on the death of a third cousin, who had left her an amethyst necklace. "A thing I couldn't wear, you know, so I sold it, and spent the produce in cypress wreaths, and immortelles, tied with black riband, with which I decorated the room and the tea-table, in the poor thing's honour ; and though we didn't have ' funeral baked meats,' we ate ' *soupirs*,' and everyone said it was charming, so original." But Grace declined the proffered honour, as she was obliged to do many other entertainments that last week.

Some twelve miles from Boston, but served by a branch railway which decants the traveller at a station hard by the gate of the grounds, stands a pleasant grey stone house of moderate size,

built by the late Mr. Richardson. That talented
architect, who struck out a new line in domestic
building, and created, it may be said, the school
of American architecture which is now so
flourishing throughout the land, never designed
a more picturesque home than this of Brackly.
The low Byzantine arch, beneath which the
front-door steps ascend, and then turn sharp
to the right hand; the heavy mullioned bay-
window, and corner turret with its sharp pin-
nacle, and wide range of outlook, over the cliffs
and down to the sea, the steep-pitched red
roof, and stone balcony thrust out from a
recessed window under another arch, the heavy
oak door with its old venetian knocker of
wrought iron, every feature is agreeable and
harmonizes. And the face of this delightful
dwelling, on the summit of a green slope, surrounded by fine beeches, is as the face of a
friend from the old world to the traveller who
has just left behind him the hideous uniformity
of city streets. The trees were still bare;
through the rich brown earth of the flower-beds
not even a crocus had as yet thrust its golden
head; but the sea beyond the sandhills was
very blue, and the log-wood down by the lake

made a spot of crimson colour against the grey green bank.

Grace lingered for an instant on the door-step.

" How lovely ! " she cried.

" There ought to be ducks there. By Jove ! I see some," said Mordy.

Then they turned into the oak-panelled hall. A curtain of old Flemish tapestry was lifted at the further end, and Mrs. Courtly, as lithe as a girl of fifteen, with a garden hat, an apron, and a pair of scissors in her hand, ran towards them.

" Welcome to Brackly ! So glad to see you both. And you have brought fine weather. It snowed yesterday, I was in despair. You like my little home ? I am so glad. It is not like your grand English places, but the view is pretty, and the house comfortable, I hope."

" There is comfort for the eyes, and comfort for the mind, I see," said Grace, looking round her, " as well as for the body."

" Those were wonderful cobs that brought us from the station," said Mordy. " I never sat behind better steppers."

" You shall sit behind something better to-morrow, Sir Mordaunt, one of our fast trotters ;

but come into the parlour, or, as you would say,
the drawing-room."

She lifted the portière again and they entered
a long apartment, with deep bay-windows, at
the further end of which was a daïs, raised upon
three steps, where stood the piano.   From this
" coyn of vantage," the view over the sandhills
to the sea was more extensive ; and here some
rocking chairs, and a table covered with books,
showed that it was a favourite corner with Mrs.
Courtly and her friends.   On the walls of this
room were a few good Italian pictures, not too
many ; one or two fine plates of Maestro
Giorgio, and Spanish lustre ware, with silver-
bound missals and ivory caskets, in an old
English glazed cabinet ; in another some rare
books.   But the place had not the air of a
curiosity-shop ; nor was the first impression
you received one of stupefaction at what it must
all have cost.   Thoroughly comfortable chairs,
the last new books and magazines, the score of
" Parsifal " upon the desk of the open piano,
these touches of modernity, and cultivation
" up to date " disarmed the Philistine who
might be disposed to charge the collector of
these treasures with æsthetic affectation.

"How charming it all is !" exclaimed Grace. "I never saw a more delightful 'Lady's Bower.' It seems as if nothing but what is refined could live here—nothing but sunshine enter those windows !"

"Ah ! it is twelve years old, it has already had its share of storm and showers." She sighed, and then turning, said, "I see you are looking at my portrait, Sir Mordaunt. It is by Michael Angelo Brown. Do you like it ?"

"No, I think it is horrid. It doesn't do you justice, Mrs. Courtly."

"And I think it masterly," said his sister. "He has caught that enigmatical expression that reminded me, when I first saw you, of Leonardo's 'Gioconda.'"

"I am pleased. You are the second person who has said that. I shall tell Brown."

"You may add also what I say," said Mordaunt, laughing, "that it doesn't do you a bit of justice."

"Oh ! you are a flatterer, and a Philistine, Sir Mordaunt. You prefer prettiness to individuality. The New School which Brown represents here, rather courts ugliness, certainly would rather have ugliness than lose individuality."

"I know. I've seen a whole lot he did of Mrs. Van Winkle. I thought them all beastly. Mrs. Van Winkle fencing, apparently in a vapour bath ; Mrs. Van Winkle yawning,—no, singing, I suppose it is, because she is at the piano, with one hand up, and her little finger stuck out at right angles with her hand. Forgive me if I say it is all so damned affected."

"You talk of what you don't understand, Mordy," said Grace, impatiently. "Both those pictures are very, *very* clever."

Mrs. Courtly gave her low rippling laugh.

"I like the fresh expression of opinion. One so seldom gets it. Mrs. Planter (you know the Planters ?) stood dumb before my portrait for a minute or two. Then she said the *chiaro 'scuro* was wonderful."

"I should like it better if it were more *chiaro* and less *oscuro*," laughed Mordaunt in reply. "Is she a fool ?"

"By no means. She is a dear woman, only she has not the courage of her opinions. She is so anxious to be amiable. They arrived this morning, and are gone up to their rooms to rest. I expect Quintin Ferrars presently, and two great friends of mine from Boston, George

Laffan, the author, and Burton, a young musician, whose compositions I think charming."

"I shall be quite out of it among all this talent!" sighed Mordaunt: and he shrugged his shoulders with a smile.

"How absurd you are, Sir Mordaunt! Is he accustomed to have compliments paid him all the time, Miss Ballinger? Is he fishing?"

"He has had too many since he landed. Don't increase the evil, Mrs. Courtly. It is quite time we went to the Wild West. In New York we both ran the risk of being spoilt."

"We shall not spoil you here," rejoined her hostess, with one of her bright smiles, "because it is what is best in you, and therefore impossible to spoil, that we Bostonians shall chiefly prize. I claim to be a Bostonian, you know, because I was born there. Ah! I see you are looking at that small picture by Jansen. Do you recognize the face? It is supposed to be Mary Stuart."

"She must have had as many heads as Cerberus," said Mordaunt, "for no two resemble each other."

"Pardon me! this is very like the one at Windsor. Next it is a Rembrandt I bought at the Demidoff sale at Florence."

"How wonderful, to make an ugly, old woman so interesting!" Grace exclaimed. "What an odd sort of battledore and shuttle-cock Art and Nature play! One would not be attracted by a face like a withered walnut, till one saw this admirable portrait. The next time one saw it in the flesh one would be delighted."

"Well, I shouldn't," said Mordaunt, moving on to a cabinet of miniatures. "I like these much better. In miniatures, they have always got such awfully nice skins—like velvet. I wish more women in real life had such com-plexions. That must have been a little duck—that woman with the powdered hair."

"Madame de Pompadour—well, she *was* a duck, in her way. She swam in troubled waters, and so did this poor bird who was more of a swan, Marie Antoinette, white and stately, with her long throat. And this is our Martha Washington, more of the barn-door fowl, and near to her, Lafayette, and further on, Franklin. I love to talk to these historic ghosts. I can

take up one of these miniatures and am carried
right back to those days. I seem to read all
their stories in those faces. But here is the
tea, and more substantial food than ghosts can
give us."

Two servants entered with trays, which they
arranged on a table, with an old Chelsea service,
out of which it was manifest one could drink
nothing but " a dish " of tea ; and a George III.
" equipage " of silver, urn-shaped kettle, and
all. Grace could have fancied herself in an old
English country house, where all had remained
unchanged for the last hundred years.

Presently the Planter ladies descended. It
was obvious that the " rest " they were credited
with having required, was an euphony for
elaborate toilette. The mother's clothes became her years ; but the daughter was so nobly
beautiful that she should have been simply
dressed. Grace, in her tight-fitting tweed, felt
no feminine envy for the gold-braided waistcoat
and velvet jacket trimmed with blue fox which
the girl wore; here, in the country, this splendour
was singularly out of place ; even in the city it
would have seemed to English ideas a little
oppressive on one so young. But the smile on

that beautiful and by no means weak face was so captivating that "the first instalment of her," as Grace afterwards expressed it, could not fail to please.

"I am so glad to meet you in the country," she said, as she sat down on the sofa next to Grace. "One knows people so much better in the country. Why would you not come to Tuxedo, when Jem Gunning asked us to meet you? We had such a good time. But it would have been ever so much better if you had come."

"It is very kind of you to say that, but I never promised Mr. Gunning to go to Tuxedo. I should have been very glad to have met you, but —I am sure this is much nicer than Tuxedo."

"Of course it is. Brackly is just like an English house, isn't it?"

"Yes, and that I see is a compliment in your eyes."

"I should think so! I love England. Do you know Wraxford? No? or Binly? This reminded me a little of Binly."

"I should have thought the duke had too many places for any of them to look as much lived in as this does. That is the advantage of having only one home."

Miss Planter looked puzzled for an instant
—not longer.

" If you fill your house full of friends all the
time, it will soon get to look lived in, I think.
You in England understand all the amusements of country life so well. We have no
country life, no hunting and shooting for the
men, to take them away from business ; so, if
we do go to the country, it's awfully slow, and
we never remain long."

" You have no interests, I suppose ? Perhaps it requires an education to feel an interest
in a village—in the school—in all the little
schemes that arise for the welfare of the poor,
in the cutting of trees, and irrigation of the
land, and gardening, and beautifying your property. Those who really love country life have
no end of interests and amusements, indepen-
dent of society."

" Well, of course I saw nothing of that quiet
sort of life. It was boating, or riding, lawn
tennis or picnics with dancing or music of an
evening, all the time."

" And is the result of your experience that
you would like to live in England ? '

" Well, I don't know. I had a very good

time there, but I am awfully fond of my own
country, my own people. I would require a
great inducement to give them up. I suppose
the truth is, it would all depend on the man.
I should want to be very much in love."

" I am glad to hear that. It is supposed to
be an antiquated idea, as much out of date
here, I suppose, as with us. But as you have
made so many friends in England, if you
return there, you are almost sure to find the
man."

" I don't know about that. Pap-pa doesn't
want me to find him in England. Mam-ma
doesn't mind, if the man has a good position."
Here she turned with her lovely smile to
Ballinger, and said, " Don't you want to give
me some tea, Sir Mordaunt ? "

As he handed the cup to her, his sister read
in his eyes that he wished for her seat by Miss
Planter ; so Grace rose, and joined the two
ladies at the tea-table. She could not help
thinking that Mrs. Courtly was just a little
bored by the conversation of the " dear woman."
The desire not to be ranked as an ordinary
Pittsburgher, but as a person belonging to the
most exclusive circles in London and New

York, was a little irritating. She could talk of
nothing else. Pittsburg was relegated to the
dust-bin of things to be swept away; though
there Père Planter was still amassing his
dollars, and, while he allowed his spouse to
spend them freely, during the greater part of
the year, constrained her to join him occasionally. Grace sat by and listened to Mrs.
Planter's small fry of gossip, floating in a shal-
low bath of sentiments, and brought to the
surface to nibble from time to time, by an
" Ah ! " or " Indeed ! " from her hostess ; much
as an indolent fisher languidly casts a net, con-
scious that the only fish to be caught are insig-
nificant and flabby.

There was a pleasant diversion, however,
before long, caused by the arrival of Messrs.
Laffan and Burton. The coming of the two
Bostonians was hailed by Mrs. Courtly with
pretty demonstrations of pleasure. She was
never afraid of showing the satisfaction she de-
rived from the presence of her men friends ;
and this frankness of demonstration was sometimes ill-naturedly commented upon by her own
sex.

Miss Ballinger had met Mr. Laffan in London.

Who had not met that gracious, elderly man of
the world, who acted so long as a social bridge
between the two countries ?   The bridge is now
broken ; others will arise in succession, but none
will ever take exactly the place of that which is
gone.   It is needless to describe one so well
known, who was always greeted with as much
warmth in London as in his native city ; it is
enough to say that in Mrs. Courtly's house he
was a special favourite, and a very constant
visitor.

Mr. Burton, on the other hand, was an unknown quantity to Grace.   She had never
before met a romantic-looking American, with
tender, dreamy eyes, and that soft, far-away
manner which indicates a mind little fit to cope
with the hard actualities of life.   He had none
of the brilliant incisiveness common to his
countrymen ; he would have been sadly at a
loss in a contest with May Clayton.   But it
was not till after dinner, when he sat down to
play, that she realized how much the man lived
in a world of his own.   He seemed to forget
that he had an audience ; he was talking to
himself, as it were, in that sweet poet's language, which only the chosen few can under-

stand. As his soliloquy rambled on, through doubt, remonstrance, despair, from plaintive elegy to wild rhapsody, two at least among his hearers were stirred, as though they were listening to the passionate struggles, the jubilant conquest of a troubled soul.

But Quintin Ferrars was not one of those to whom music speaks. He had arrived very late, and Grace had not seen him till just before dinner. At table the conversation was general, but later he sat down by Grace, who was next the piano, and began talking, regardless of the fact that Burton was playing. Twice Grace placed her finger on her lips, the third time, Mrs. Courtly came up and shook her fan at him.

"You bad man! If you want to talk, you must go into the next room."

"Won't you come, Miss Ballinger?" he said. "Your brother and Miss Planter are there. That will equalize the company."

" I am sorry for their want of taste. I prefer listening to Mr. Burton."

Ferrars said nothing, but retired to a distant corner of the room, and took up the *Century*. He spoke to no one during the

remainder of the evening.   Mrs. Planter murmured at proper intervals that it was truly
delightful, so intellectual, so metaphysical
(she pronounced it mutterphysical).   Mrs.
Courtly and Grace scarcely spoke, but silence
is often more eloquent than words, and in his
hostess, at least, the young musician knew he
had a listener who understood what it was he
meant to say.   It was this power of understanding which made Mrs. Courtly a delightful
companion to so many and to such very
different sorts of people.

CHAPTER XII.

THE next day was Sunday, and when the party assembled at breakfast at half-past nine, it appeared that Mrs. Courtly had already been to early Communion, at the neighbouring church.

"The carriage will be here at eleven for anyone who wants to go to morning service. I am going to Evensong instead, and shall take Mr. Laffan for a drive this morning. What will you do, Miss Ballinger ? "

Grace said she wished to go to church, whereupon Miss Planter declared she meant to go also, adding,—

" I hear Samuel Sparks is near here, and will probably preach."

" Yes," said Mrs Courtly. " That is the reason I am not going."

" Is he not a very great preacher ? ' asked Grace.

"Yes, but I do not consider him orthodox. He is too broad in his views to suit me."

Grace had been under a vague impression that all American religion was "broad:" she had no idea that a section of the community cherished a rigid ritualism.

"Samuel Sparks is a lovely man," said Mrs. Planter, shaking her head gently, "but perhaps a little *too*—"

Her criticism was left to shift for itself as best it might, in the minds of her hearers. All the men had heard the famous preacher except Sir Mordaunt, and he was not a very regular church-goer. However, on this occasion, he declared that his curiosity was fired, he would accompany the ladies. Mrs. Courtly smiled blandly across the silver urn at him.

"Mrs. Van Winkle will no longer be able to compare you to Guy Livingston. I am glad you go to church. *You*, I know, Quintin, are past praying for—"

"Quite." He cut her short, decisively.

"In England it is thought good form for men to go to church. They did so when we stayed in county houses there all the time," said Mrs. Planter.

"All the time?" repeated Sir Mordaunt interrogatively, with a look of amused wonder.

"Mam-ma means every Sunday," explained her daughter; then added laughing,—"All, except a few old heathens, politicians, and philosophers, and people who buried themselves in the library."

"I am not a politician, but I hope I am a philosopher," said Ferrars, with a tolerant smile.

"I am neither one nor the other," sighed Burton, with an appealing look at Mrs. Courtly. "But when the music is bad, my soul is in revolt, it makes me so cross. I go away worse than I came. And the music in your church here is very bad—you know it is, Mrs. Courtly."

So the three drove off to church together. Nothing in the service invited comment (the music being no worse than the Ballingers were used to in their own country church), until Mr. Sparks began to read the first lesson. He had not opened his lips till then. Apparently there was a storage of sound waiting to escape, and it rushed forth with a volubility truly astounding. Ballinger looked at his sister with elevated brows. It was clear that the minister expected the congregation to be conversant with the text of Holy Writ; otherwise it was impossible to follow him. He read also a portion of the Communion service in a manner that seemed to Grace little short of irreverent. But all this was as nothing compared to the rapidity of his utterance when he reached the pulpit. His sermon was a splendid piece of oratory, charged with noble thought, clad in language that seemed, like lightning, to strike and tear the ground. Then, as the thunder rolled along, the scorn of self-seeking and of sloth, the denunciation of envy and uncharitableness, fell like hail smiting the consciences of some who heard. But the electric rapidity with which the words poured down was such that, as flash succeeded flash, many of the congregation were blinded, groping their way feebly, and clutching at his meaning here and there. It required long usage (and to some of those assembled he was almost a stranger), or a sharp, retentive vision, not to be dazzled as the lightning struck peak after peak, and the wind swept by, and the great storm drove on relentless, without pause or hesitation.

Miss Planter only removed her beautiful eyes from the preacher, to glance surreptitiously, from time to time, at her companions, and judge of the effect produced on them. Grace listened, eager and absorbed ; her brother gnawed his moustache, and looked ill at ease. When, at last, the torrent of words stopped, and the congregation slid out of church, in various mental conditions, the American girl's curiosity found its vent.

"Well ?" she asked, addressing Mordaunt. "What do you say ? Is he not just wonderful ?"

"Wonderful ! I believe you. I never heard a chap pour out so many words to the minute before. It's perfectly awful, going on like this, for more than half an hour without stopping !"

"How I wished I could write shorthand !" exclaimed his sister. " It is too sad to think it is all gone beyond recall. I never heard anything so splendid, so stirring ! "

" I am awfully glad you think so," said Miss Planter, who clung fondly to the English slang she had acquired. " I hoped that you, Sir Mordaunt, would have felt a little moved. Samuel Sparks always *does* move me so ! "

" Move me ! Why, I felt as if I were being hurled down a precipice, and were clutching wildly at twigs, roots, anything to save myself. But it was no use; as fast as I caught hold of anything, it slipped from me, and I felt just as if I'd come an awful cropper, bruised and stunned when he stopped."

The conversation was renewed at luncheon, when Mrs. Courtly expressed a desire to know how her English guests had been impressed by the famous preacher. Her feelings as a patriotic American and a staunch Churchwoman were divided. Miss Ballinger satisfied one sentiment, Sir Mordaunt the other.

" As far as I could make out," he said, "it was more of a lecture than a sermon. But then I made out very little."

" Whatever it was, it was exceedingly fine," said his sister, with decision. " I have come to the conclusion that Americans are much more eloquent than Englishmen. We have no orator in either House to compare with Mr. Sparks."

" A preacher has every other sort of orator at a disadvantage," said Ferrars, grimly. " He

can say what he likes, he can scourge you,
without fear of reprisal."

"Yes," said Mrs. Courtly, "and there must
have been many present, who—like myself—
object, not only to Mr. Sparks' manner, but to
his doctrine. His ability is undoubted, of
course."

"How is it, Mrs. Courtly, that he comes to
be preaching in a ritualistic church?" asked
Grace.

"In former years the division was very great.
Doctrine was paramount, before eloquence, or
anything. Latterly there has been a growing
tendency to let pastors of different views change
pulpits. It is a practice I do not care about,
but I suppose its has it advantages."

"If people *will* be preached at," said Ferrars,
"it is better that the subject should be looked
at from different points of view, with more
freedom and liberty than from the narrow plane
of one parsonic mind."

"Oh, my! Mr. Ferrars," exclaimed Mrs.
Planter, "why should ministers have narrower
minds than anyone else?"

"I did not say they had. All minds looking
at one subject from one point of view become

narrow. I know mine has," he muttered.
Then, with a satirical smile, "And yours. Like
a good mother, it is concentrated on your
daughter, and I am sure you only take one view
of her future. You can't take an all-round
survey of the position."

Mrs. Planter bristled; she did not know how
to receive this odd speech. As she said afterwards to Mrs. Courtly, "It was so very—"

But her amiable hostess threw herself into
the breach. With a smile at the girl, who was
colouring, "There can be but one view of
Clare's future," she said quickly. "She has
already most of the good things of this world.
She will find the best, and be clever enough to
know when she has found it."

It was a clear, still afternoon, though very
cold. The recent snow had left the roads
ankle-deep in slush, which there had been
neither frost, nor wind, the previous day to dry.
Now it was freezing, but not hard enough to
affect the mud to any depth. The road on
which all the party set out to walk was certainly
very bad; it would have been difficult to match
it in any country district in England; but then,
they did not walk on the road. The system,

unknown with us, of laying down planks on the wayside for pedestrians, secured them a dry foot-path. But only two could walk abreast. Mr. Burton had timidly endeavoured to place himself beside Grace ; Ferrars' dominant perseverance however secured that privilege.

" You behaved very ill, last night, Mr. Ferrars," began Miss Ballinger, with her characteristic fearlessness, " and again to-day at luncheon. You sulked, because you were not allowed to talk, and because I wanted to listen to the music ; and to-day you attacked poor Mrs. Planter in a most unjustifiable way."

" I am not aware that I attacked her. I said her thoughts were concentrated on her daughter's future—"

" You know very well what you meant ; and *she* knew. Cynics like you are always crying out against the follies and weakness of the world ; and you have just as many yourselves. It is Hudibras over again, what you are ' inclined to ;' and what you ' have no mind to.' "

" I daresay you are right," he returned, with unusual gentleness ; " but if you knew how the world has treated me, you would be more lenient in your judgment, you would understand how

I have come to be misanthropic and bitter.
Perhaps some day you may know."

She felt sorry for him ; she liked the man,
with all his faults ; perhaps she was not
superior to the womanly love of influence over
one whom few attracted. But her clear sense
prevented her being blinded by the sophism
of his defence ; and she said impulsively,—

"You expect leniency, but you show none.
And, then, you are like a spoilt child, sulking,
as you did last night—or running away, as you
did more than once in New York, because
somebody came into the room you did not like !
I think suffering ought to make men stronger,
not weaker, Mr. Ferrars."

"You are severe, but you don't understand—
you can't." He beat the long, yellow grass,
that sprang up beside the planks, with the
blackthorn in his hand. "If I were under your
influence always," he added, in a low voice, "I
should become more tolerant, I believe. I
should look at things from a different point of
view."

"Oh ! If I were your sister," laughed Miss
Ballinger, "I should lecture you. I should
keep you in better order. As it is, I can't

think, judging by your conduct, that my presence has a very beneficial effect."

"Perhaps not at the time ; it marks the contrast more strongly." He paused a moment ;
how could he explain his feelings without
startling her ? And yet he felt some explanation of this enigmatical sentence was needed.
"You see," he continued, "I have avoided
society for years. I suppose I have become
brutalized ; I have lost the habit of concealing
what I think, or doing what bores me. When
I see you with such people as the Hurlstones,
or Mrs. Van Winkle, or these Planters, my con-
tempt of the world is increased. I want to
talk to you or to go right away. If I enter into
general conversation, I am sure to say something which will offend them."

"So little self-restraint ? That comes from
having shut yourself away from people, and
having had your own way too long. All the
men I have heard you speak so slightingly of,
because they devote their whole time and
energies to amassing big fortunes, lead really
healthier lives than you do. They rub up
against all manner of people ; they give and
take."

"They take more than they give," he said, with a sneer; "and because they rub up against all manner of people, they become callous. Is it well to become callous? to grow indifferent— almost blind to evil? to pass through life shrugging one's shoulders? Well, perhaps it is. And, yet, I've had enough to make me callous. But one can't alter one's nature."

"That is the defence of everyone who gives in," she returned. "And it is horribly weak —quite unworthy of a man, *I* think. I am a great hero-worshipper, and all my heroes fight something—either their own passions, or something else they are resolved to conquer. And, as to growing callous, I don't see that anyone need become so because he mixes with his fellow-creatures, even the very worst. We have a Great Example of that; and all the devoted workers among the poor of big cities do not lose their sense of right and wrong because they are pitiful and forbearing."

Here Mrs. Courtly, who was in front, turned round. They had reached the village, or rather small agglomeration of houses of the lower middle class, as we should denominate them, which were clustered around the church.

The bell was ringing; one or two elderly women, a young girl, a pale-faced man carrying some books, were hurrying along. Mrs. Courtly said,—

" Here I leave you ; and I give Mr. Laffan into your charge, Miss Ballinger. What! Quintin, are you coming with me to church ? Well, wonders will never cease. Good-bye, all of you, till tea-time."

And so the bright, genial little lady, with her unwonted escort, left the rest of the party to find their own way home.

Quintin Ferrars had not entered a church for years. What prompted him to leave Grace, and accompany his friend ? Was it the girl's words ? Was it Mr. Laffan's joining her ? Was it some inexplicable working of conscience ?

END OF VOL I.

www.ingramcontent.com/pod-product-compliance
Lightning Source LLC
Chambersburg PA
CBHW030114030726
47498CB00007B/2372